Pistol Perfect

Pink Pistol Sisterhood Series Book Eleven

Jessie Gussman

Published By: Jessie Gussman

Contents

Acknowledgments

Cover art by Julia Gussman
Editing by Heather Hayden
Author Services by CE Author Assistant

Enjoy incredible audio performances of **75+ *unabridged Jessie Gussman books for FREE*** by Jay Dyess on the Say with Jay channel on YouTube.

Chapter 1

"Are you sure that's solid?" Mabel Lefrak eyed the barnyard muck dubiously.

As a large animal vet, she didn't notice the tangy smell of cow manure that hung heavy in the air, but she'd been in her share of mucky places, and to her at least, the slop in Carol Smith's barnyard looked like it could swallow a person whole.

"Yes. I'm quite sure. I had my nephew put that box in the shed last fall. He walked right over without any problems."

There was a difference in precipitation between the fall and spring seasons in North Dakota, which could have a rather large impact on whether Mabel was able to walk across it, or whether she got sucked into Middle Earth.

But Carol had mentioned she had an antique that quite possibly had belonged to the great Annie Oakley. Animals might be Mabel's first love, but anything Annie Oakley was a close second. She just hadn't been able to figure out how to make a living by reading and studying about the famed sharpshooter. So she became a vet instead.

That made as much sense as pretty much everything else in her life so far.

"All right. If you say so," Mabel said, even though the reason she chose to proceed had more to do with getting her hands on something Annie might have touched and less on Carol Smith's word that the ground between the edge of the barn where they currently stood and the shed that housed the box was solid.

Not that she didn't trust Carol. After all, she'd agreed to move in with her to help her out until her nephew was able to move in or, from what Mabel understood, move her out, since the nephew had a business in Chicago and she couldn't imagine he'd want to move to North Dakota.

"I'm sure you'll be fine."

Famous last words. Except they weren't as Mabel picked her way carefully over the cushy but firm ground.

It didn't help that Billy, the Highland steer who typically hung out in the town of Sweet Water but, for some reason, had chosen to visit Carol today, stood in a spot where his hooves had sunk in so the mud was up to his knees.

"What are you doing here, Billy?" Mabel said as she moved past him. She'd have to ask Carol after she made it back. Billy didn't really belong to anyone. The whole town took care of him, and in return, he brought in tourism dollars, since he'd developed a bit of a reputation as a matchmaking steer.

"You're wasting your time here," Mabel murmured. But Billy didn't seem to care and kept on chewing his cud, his eyes half-closed.

She wished she were as calm as he was, but she couldn't shake the feeling that the mud in the barnyard was a lot deeper than anyone thought and that one wrong step would have her sinking up to her armpits.

She had to breathe a sigh of relief when she made it to the storage shed. She'd never actually heard of anyone getting stuck in a barnyard and needing to be pulled out by a crane or something, but she'd watched cows step through mud up to their underbellies and a farmer that she'd worked with once had lost an entire boot in deep muck.

Still, all she had to do was grab the box and walk back and she could say she survived.

Opening the door of the shed, she peered in.

"There aren't any lights," Carol called from her—safe—spot on the other side of the barnyard.

"Okay," Mabel called, distracted. The shed was piled floor to ceiling with boxes and bags and oddly shaped items that looked like they'd been packed in by a professional. Not a centimeter of space was wasted.

"It's on the right. It's about this big"

Mabel looked over her shoulder. Carol had her hands up, indicating the box wasn't super huge. She turned back around, looking for something about that size on her right.

Stacks of boxes and some things covered with a sheet met her gaze as it slid sideways. She bit down on her lips, squinting in the dim light, her heart beating just a touch faster than normal. She could be within seconds of touching something that once belonged to Annie Oakley.

There. On top of a pile of boxes, uncovered, alone, a deep mahogany rectangular box resided, almost like a queen on her throne.

Reigning over a barnyard of muck and a shed full of...whatever a person who was almost seventy took with them when they moved from Oklahoma to North Dakota.

Mabel stepped toward the box, picking it up reverently. Annie Oakley could have touched this very box.

Almost overcome by curiosity about what, exactly, was in the box, she resisted the urge. She couldn't open it without Carol.

Instead, she tucked it carefully under her arm and walked out of the shed, closing the large wooden door carefully behind her. If the things were worth moving from Oklahoma to North Dakota, they were worth taking the time to make sure the door was closed and they wouldn't be exposed to the elements.

Maybe it was her excitement over the box, or maybe it was the fact that Billy had moved a little to the left from where he'd been standing and she didn't notice it right away. Maybe it was just something that was bound to happen.

Whatever it was, Mabel took a slightly different path through the barnyard on the way back from the shed. An unfortunate decision on her part since she was just a little over halfway through when she took a step...and the ground gave way beneath her foot.

Mabel's stomach dropped like a hot potato, and she let out a yelp, automatically moving her other foot forward to try to catch her fall.

Pointless, since that foot sank deeply into the wet manure as well.

Manure wasn't quicksand, but for some reason, that's where Mabel's mind went as she frantically tried to pull her feet out. She'd heard that if a person fell into quicksand, the more they struggled, the deeper and faster they sank.

But how could she not try to get herself out?

Clutching the box—she wasn't going to survive man-eating manure only to lose her treasure—she pulled up on first one leg, then another, the manure sucking and grasping at her feet.

She leaned forward and put her free hand on the ground in front of her, her heart pounding and her breath coming in shallow gasps. If only Billy could talk. She'd ask him to give her a horn and pull her out.

Pausing for a fraction of a second to gather her strength, she pulled as hard as she could and her foot popped up.

Her shoe did not.

Ugh. She didn't want to lose her shoe.

Still holding tight to the box, she was able to pull her other foot out, a layer of manure an inch thick sticking like a clay blanket to her entire lower leg and foot, but at least her shoe remained in its proper position on her foot.

On her hand and knees, she turned, shoving her free arm down into the hole where her first leg had been, fishing blindly around in the muck, trying to feel anything that could be her shoe.

She had her arm in up to her armpit and couldn't feel anything except the surprisingly cool muck.

The stench was overpowering, even for someone used to working in barnyards all across central North Dakota.

Something touched her from behind, and she fell forward. Unwilling to let go of the box to catch herself, she managed to turn her head so she landed with her left cheek in the muck. What in the world?

Twisting her head, she saw a big, furry body innocently standing directly behind her. It must have been Billy, trying to scratch his head on her rear end, which had probably been sticking up in the air a good bit higher than he was used to seeing rear ends stick, that had pushed her forward.

She could hardly get upset with him. Billy was as sweet and good-natured as a cow could be.

Still, she wasn't really feeling any goodwill toward him as she pushed herself—carefully—to her feet, manure covering practically every inch of her front from her head down to her exposed toes.

"Thanks, Billy," she muttered, more than a little sarcastically, as she turned, intending to stomp the rest of the way across the barnyard.

But she hadn't even taken a step before she stopped short.

A man, tall with deep blue eyes, stood in front of her, and if she were any judge, his lips were pressed tightly together to keep from laughing at her.

She probably was a sight, but it still irritated.

But she had to give the man credit. He did not smile, although he did not offer to shake, either, as he introduced himself. "I'm James, Carol's nephew."

It could have been her imagination, but it felt like, at his words, the box under her arm vibrated.

Odd.

Chapter 2

J ames stared at Mabel.

She didn't recognize him. He'd wondered over the years if she would remember him when he came back. He'd been tempted to come back much earlier, just because of that fear—that she'd forget him, or that she'd never noticed him to begin with. But he knew she had been working toward getting her degree and becoming a practicing vet.

He kept tabs on her as well as he could. Without being a creepy stalker.

Of course, considering that she was covered in cow manure from her feet, one of which didn't have a shoe, to the top of her head, with very little space on her body that wasn't dirty, it was rather astounding that he was the one worried about *her* liking *him*.

Even though she was filthy...the years he'd waited had been worth it.

That was the thought that was running through his head as he held his hand out.

She looked down at both of hers, which were covered in mud, and then looked back with a sheepish expression on her face. "Sorry, I don't think you want to shake right now, but I'm Mabel."

He nodded, tempted to say, "I know," but he didn't. He didn't want to tip his hand. Instead, he allowed his hand to drop and said, "I understand you just moved in with my aunt."

"You're the nephew," she said, and she sounded a little breathless. Maybe from having just gotten stuck in the barnyard muck, or...could it be something else?

He tried to shove that thought aside, because he knew he really wanted to believe that there could be something between them.

He'd fallen for her years ago, when she was way too young and his business wasn't established.

Then her parents had died, and she had continued on to vet school.

"I should have introduced you two. I didn't realize you didn't know James. I thought you did." Aunt Carol hurried over with a tea towel in her hand.

The towel was no match for the dirt on Mabel's face, but she took it from Aunt Carol gladly, with a smile, and started wiping at the worst of the muck.

"You know, James used to work with your father."

Mabel froze, the towel covering her face as she had been swiping at something on her forehead.

Her knuckles whitened, just for a second, and then she finished dabbing at her forehead and the towel slowly lowered.

"I remember you now." There was a betrayal in her eyes, like she was upset with him for not mentioning that, but her gaze was direct and maybe a little curious. Nothing more.

He tried to make sure he looked casual and not like he'd orchestrated the entire thing.

All except for the muck that currently covered her.

And the box she still held under her armpit.

"Yeah. You used to tag along with your dad on some of his business trips. Always with your nose in a book. I think he hoped that bringing you would encourage you to be more social, but it seemed to have the opposite effect."

He shouldn't be saying stuff like that. He didn't mean to insult her. But he found her desire to hide in the corner with a good book cute and endearing. And it had made him curious about her. The quiet girl who sat in the corner. The one most people overlooked. She didn't seem to be sad or upset that she was ignored; in fact, that seemed to be what she wanted. She always left as soon as her father would excuse her to go back to their room.

It didn't surprise him at all that she had become a vet, although he supposed that while vets worked with animals, they worked with people just as much. After all, every animal they worked on was owned by a person.

"Dad tried." Mabel smiled sadly. When he'd shown up after her parents had died, Gladys had been handling things just fine with the tall man at her elbow, and to his disappointment, he knew he wouldn't be needed. Still, he heard that the family hadn't been very close, and he'd also heard that the girls had been left in some financial difficulties after the parents passed away.

He funneled some money to them, through various means, making sure that it wouldn't be tracked. He didn't want Mabel to want him for his money. He'd been born into a wealthy family, and all of his life, people had wanted to be his friends based on his wealth. He knew how fickle friendships built on money could be.

If Mabel didn't love him for who he was, as hard as it was to face, he would rather not have her.

A ringtone burst into the stillness of the midmorning air. Mabel jumped and then said, "That's mine. Excuse me. It could be an emergency."

She shifted the box under her arm, careful not to get it dirty, and pulled her phone out of her pocket, finding a clean spot on her shirt to wipe it before she answered.

"Hello," she said, turning her shoulder toward them and looking partially away. "Oh. Yeah." There was a small pause, and then she said, "I'll be right there."

She swiped off her phone and shoved it back in her pocket, turning back to Aunt Carol and him.

"I'm sorry. I have to leave. I..." She fumbled a little with the box, handing it toward Aunt Carol. "I really want to see what's in this, but I want to do it sometime when I have a little bit more time."

"That's just fine," Aunt Carol said, taking the box from Mabel and holding it carefully, gently, like there was something valuable in it. "If you get back in time tonight, we can sit in the living room and look at it. I imagine James will be here, although he hasn't told me how long he is staying this time."

"Is my living here going to be a problem?" Mabel asked, looking at him with concern.

Not at all.

"Of course not. My aunt wanted to keep the house for me, but she didn't want to stay here by herself. I'm glad she found a roommate."

He didn't mention that he was considering moving back on a permanent basis, and not necessarily just because of Aunt Carol, although he would have considered it anyway, even without Mabel. Aunt Carol was childless, and he had taken upon himself the responsibility of caring for her. She might not realize it, but she was getting up in years, and he really did think she shouldn't be living by herself.

Still, it was an excuse to come back to Sweet Water.

Mabel hurried off, and he knew he shouldn't, but he watched her go. She used the towel Aunt Carol had brought to wipe herself off the best she could, but then she pulled a sheet out of the back of her car and threw it over her seat, like it was something that she'd done multiple times before.

Probably, as a veterinarian, she had left more than one place covered in the same stuff she was covered in now. So it would stand to reason that she was prepared.

Of course, she probably hadn't expected to have that happen today.

"What's up with the box?" He finally turned to Aunt Carol as the back of Mabel's car disappeared down the road.

Aunt Carol smiled with a little bit of smugness, James would have said. "I got this from someone when I lived in Oklahoma. It's supposed to be...not magical, but...there's something about it. Something different."

"Something different. Okay. What is it?" James tamped down his impatience. Aunt Carol's eyes shone, and she looked excited, but she hadn't even told him what was in the box.

"It's something that used to belong to Annie Oakley, from what I understand. It's...helped others. And I thought maybe it would help you."

"But you're giving it to Mabel." He didn't understand. Maybe he had misunderstood. Maybe Aunt Carol hadn't been giving it to Mabel but just showing it to her.

He felt confused.

"I was. Giving it to Mabel."

"But it's supposed to help me?"

"We'll see," Aunt Carol said enigmatically.

James pressed his lips together, holding in the other questions that wanted to tumble out. There was no point in asking Aunt Carol for answers if she was determined not to give them. He supposed things would just have to play out, but... It almost sounded like she was on his side. His side being the side that got Mabel and him together.

Maybe that was too far of a stretch.

He needed to let go of that idea.

"James, tell me how your trip was," Aunt Carol said as she slipped her arm in the crook of his elbow, and they turned and started walking toward the house.

He did love the old house. It was white, and big for North Dakota standards. Hard and expensive to heat in the winter, but with the high ceilings and spacious rooms, it was bright and felt airy and welcoming. He'd snatched it up years ago when it had fallen into disrepair, and over the years, he had it fixed up. Always intending to come back. Hoping anyway. Thinking that someday maybe he and Mabel would share it together.

Seeing her today had not made him want her any less, but she had been the same as she always was—didn't really notice him, didn't seem the slightest bit interested in him, and he had been the same as he always was, unable to find any of the charm that came so easily with everyone else.

Why couldn't he find the smooth words and casual compliments that rolled off his tongue with his casual acquaintances and friends?

Mabel always seemed to do that to him. Render him tongue-tied.

He told Aunt Carol about his trip, which wasn't anything to write home about, and then explained he had been overseeing the company as he passed the reins on to someone else, with everything going smoothly. So far.

"That's wonderful! Then you're going to stay here?" Aunt Carol asked.

"Maybe for a bit. I...don't want to make you and Mabel uncomfortable."

"Oh, you won't. Mabel won't be here much anyway, she works a lot and helps a lot with the teen girls they have at their girls' home. It took a little bit of persuading for me to convince her that I needed someone to stay with me."

He felt a little bit of panic at her words. Maybe Mabel would want to move back if he was here on a regular basis taking care of Aunt Carol.

Maybe he could feel her out, and if Aunt Carol's assessment was accurate, he would just have to make sure that he stayed away enough to make Mabel feel like she had to stay.

She had a soft heart, he knew that much about her, and if Aunt Carol needed someone to stay with her, Mabel would not leave her.

That eased his mind as they continued walking toward the house.

"Maybe you should talk to Silas, Mabel's brother-in-law. Mabel's a bit of an enigma, just because she's so quiet and keeps to herself, but she also has a ready laugh and a soft heart. You could do a lot worse."

James stopped short, one foot on the bottom porch step. He tilted his head and looked at Aunt Carol.

"What?" He had never told anyone about his fascination with Mabel. No one. He hadn't wanted to scare her off. She seemed like the kind of woman who wouldn't want a man chasing after her, that having someone who was there asking her to go out every time she turned around would make her run.

He hadn't figured out what he could do to win her, but letting her know that he was interested was probably the last thing he should do.

He wasn't sure what made him think that, but it had made him be very, very careful.

"You've loved Mabel for years, maybe even a decade. Most likely since before she had even graduated from high school." Aunt Carol stopped with him, and she put the hand that wasn't holding the box on her ample hip. "Am I wrong?"

"I don't understand how you knew." There was no point in denying the truth. He wouldn't want to lie, but he'd never had anyone confront him like this.

"Remember, I've been like a mother to you since you lost your own mother so young."

She had been his mother's oldest sister. There had been almost twenty years between them, and from what he understood, she had practically raised his own mother.

But then, his mom had been killed by a drunk driver while walking out of a restaurant.

He'd barely been ten.

But Aunt Carol had stepped in. While she didn't get along very well with his dad, who had married again, twice more, she had provided a stable home for him, opening up her home for him to stay anytime, especially during the summers.

But he hadn't seen her much since he graduated from high school. Doing what he supposed most kids did, determined to make his own mark in the world, despite the money that he'd been born with.

He'd managed to do that, at least managed to build a successful company, but from the first time he'd seen Mabel, she had been in the back of his mind, and he'd always known that he was going to come and try to win her heart.

He just didn't know how.

"I don't know how to do it. She...seems immune to me."

"Maybe that's because, if today was any indication, you seem to be tongue-tied when you're around her. Remember, I've seen your charming side, and it's pretty irresistible."

"Mabel doesn't seem like the kind of woman who is won by charm." She seemed like the kind of woman who wanted substance. Who cared about a man's character. Wanted a man who kept his word and did what he said he was going to do; a man who had integrity and honesty, and compassion and empathy.

Maybe that's just the kind of man he thought she deserved. Someone who was perfect. Someone who was not him. Probably the reason he felt tongue-tied around her was because he didn't feel like he was good enough.

"Think about what I said. Silas probably knows her better than anyone, and he might be able to give you a few tips."

"I wouldn't want to go there and have him tell the whole town how I feel. I'm pretty sure that would not help my case."

"I know Silas, and he's not that kind of man. He's the kind of man who can keep his mouth shut."

"I'm sure he can. I'm just not sure he will." He didn't know Silas very well. The last time he talked to him had been when Mabel's parents died, which was six years ago.

"I think you can trust him. But if you're not sure, go there with something else to talk about, and then you don't have to bring Mabel up if you don't feel comfortable."

That seemed like a crazy idea, and he had zero desire to go.

But Mabel was worth exploring—and doing—some crazy ideas.

"What am I going to go talk to him about? He's a mechanic. And while I appreciate what he does, I'm not in need of a mechanic."

"Aren't you?" Aunt Carol raised her brows.

He stared at her. What in the world was she trying to insinuate?

"That farm truck hasn't worked for a while now, and I'd really love to get it going again."

He opened his mouth to tell her she had just moved in less than a year ago, but he closed it.

Looking around, he saw an old clunker parked beside the barn. He snorted. "If anyone can get that thing going, it would be a miracle."

"Maybe Silas needs to tell you that. After all, you're not a mechanic."

James shook his head. He couldn't believe he was even considering doing this. He had plenty of money, and if they needed a farm truck, he could buy six of them. He didn't need Silas to come fix the dinosaur beside the barn.

But for Mabel...

"I don't suppose you have his number?" James asked, half thinking that Aunt Carol was going to whip her phone out and grab Silas's contact info off the top of her list.

He was only a little surprised when she did exactly that.

"I thought you might be asking about it, so last time I was in town, I made sure I got it."

He outright laughed at that. "You do have his number. I guess I'm not surprised for some reason."

"I figured out from the way you talk to me on the phone about her, that there might be something going on between the two of you. After all, I do believe it was your suggestion that I ask someone, and then you might have mentioned a veterinarian who lived in the area, who didn't have a house of her own and who might be looking for a place. I found that suspicious enough that it put my antenna up, and I paid attention when you talked about her. After that, it wasn't hard to figure out."

He supposed he wasn't as subtle as he thought he was being. It made him want to go regroup and figure out how he could do better.

Except, Aunt Carol had helped him; she'd given him the idea of Silas, which he had to admit was a good one.

But he still wasn't sure what to say to Silas. It wasn't a normal conversation to have with someone you'd barely ever spoken with.

"If you don't mind, I think I might stand out here and make the call."

"Of course not," Aunt Carol said, smiling at him, before she put a hand on the banister and carefully clutched the box to her chest as she walked the rest of the way up the porch steps.

He watched until she disappeared inside the house. She'd been good to him, and she was probably the one person in the world that he knew for sure loved him not because of his money.

To his surprise, Silas answered the phone on the second ring. He wasn't sure why he was expecting to leave a message, but hearing the deep voice on the other end of the line made him realize that he had no idea what he was going to say.

"Hello?"

"Is this Silas Powers?"

"It is."

"This is James Mannon, and I have...what might seem like an odd question."

"All right. Shoot." If Silas recognized his name, he didn't give any indication.

"I have an old truck out here beside the barn at the house I own outside of Sweet Water. Maybe you know my Aunt Carol. She moved in last year."

"I've heard of her. Actually, my wife's sister just moved in with her, and she seems like a nice lady from what people say in town."

"Good to know she has a good reputation." Hopefully that helped the family name around Sweet Water. Or at least in Silas's estimation, because he needed Silas's help.

"She does. In fact, I think the ladies at the community center were hoping she would join them for their crafting times."

"She hadn't said anything about that." James cleared his throat. They hadn't talked about much of anything other than Mabel. "Anyway, about this old truck."

"Is it the 1967 model Ford that's parked beside the barn?" Silas asked.

"Yes, I think. If that one is blue. How did you know?"

"I helped your aunt move in. She stored a bunch of stuff in the shed at the other end of the barnyard. I was helping the people who were carrying it in. I noticed the truck, of course. It's a classic."

"Well, that's exactly what I was calling about. I was wondering what it would take to restore it." He thought those were the right words. Restore?

There was a short silence. "Wow. I didn't look under the hood or anything, but the body would need some work. Parts would be hard to find. Might have to improvise." Silas seemed to be talking to himself, as though calculating in his head what all he would need to do. "I can't give you any guarantees, but I can come look at it if you want me to."

"I'd love it if you would." He'd much rather talk to him face-to-face. He could judge a reaction better from his body language and his facial expressions, the same way he did in the boardroom, which made him able to figure out which people needed a little extra convincing to get them to do what he wanted them to.

It wasn't something he did consciously, but it was something he picked up. His dad said it had made him a good businessman, but he hadn't wanted to use it against people, just for the right reasons.

Unfortunately, he'd seen too many people use manipulation as a legitimate tool to get what they wanted.

It had soured him on so much of what happened in business.

Shaking that thought away, he agreed with Silas when Silas suggested that he come out later today, and they hung up.

His hand dropped, and he stared at the pickup that somehow was his link to Mabel.

He didn't have much interest in old vehicles, and the idea of restoring an old pickup hadn't ever been something on his radar.

But if it would help him with Mabel... He supposed he could learn to be interested in pretty much anything.

Chapter 3

"Thank you so much for coming right away," Lark said as Mabel walked in the house.

Lark had her laptop open on the counter, and she scrolled with one hand while she absently stirred something on the stove with her other.

Lark was the busiest person Mabel knew.

Beyond having a thriving veterinary practice, she had opened her home to any girl that needed some structure and stability in their life.

At any one time, Lark was liable to have up to five girls living with her.

Mabel had actually moved out, which gave Lark another bed, although it also made things a little bit more difficult for her, since Mabel was another adult in the home and able to handle things when Lark was out on call.

"All right, I have about ten minutes, if you have that much time to talk to me?" Lark said, closing her laptop, shutting the stove off, and moving the pan away from the hot burner. "Oh, my goodness! What happened to you?" Lark said as she got a good look at Mabel for the first time and saw the manure that clung to her everywhere.

"It's a long story, but it has to do with Carol Smith and something she wanted me to get. The barnyard wasn't quite as firm as what she thought it was, and Billy was there."

"Billy?" Lark's head jerked up, her body growing still.

"Yes, Billy, but you don't have to worry about him matching me up with anyone. He did this to me." She held her arms up, showing all of the manure that had started to dry on her person.

"Interesting," Lark said, and a corner of her mouth twitched.

"I have as much time as you need," Mabel said. "But if you don't mind, I'm going to run upstairs and change my clothes first." She had left an emergency stash of clothes there just in case Lark needed her to stay with the girls anytime. She should have changed before she left Carol's house, but she hadn't thought of it. It must have been because of falling. It certainly wasn't because of seeing James.

"I don't mind at all. And you...might want to throw those away."

That was saying something coming from Lark. Normally she was very frugal.

Lark was on call this weekend, and Mabel wasn't supposed to have to work until Monday. So as long as Lark didn't get called out, they should have time to chat.

Although, if they had two calls at the same time, if she was available, even on her weekend off, she always went out.

Mabel ran upstairs and changed her clothes as quickly as she could, taking Lark's advice and throwing the clothes she took off into a garbage bag.

She threw it to the side to throw away later and went running down the steps, curious as to what Lark would have to say.

She came into the kitchen as Lark put some tea towels away.

"The girls are out feeding the animals right now, so we have a little bit of privacy. I didn't want them to hear this. I... I wanted to talk to you first."

"All right," Mabel said, grabbing glasses when she saw that Lark was getting a container of tea out of the refrigerator.

She put them on the table, filled them up, and put the container back in the refrigerator.

"You can go ahead and sit down."

"You're making me nervous," Mabel said with a smile. Lark was one of the best people she knew. Always happy, always willing to do whatever it took to serve other people. And she served them with a smile.

Mabel knew there was some type of tragedy in Lark's past, that she had had a great love of her life, but she had lost it. But to see Lark, one would never guess.

She was close with her family, the Strykers of Sweet Water, and her brothers often came around and helped when things needed to be fixed.

Mabel had never met a happier, more supportive family, and she admired Mrs. Stryker for raising her kids mostly as a single parent after her husband had passed away.

Of course, Mabel figured if people made God the center of their family, things would almost have to turn out. And that's what happened with the Strykers.

She settled into her chair while Lark fingered the back of hers.

Lark usually had trouble relaxing. She always seemed to be on the move. Maybe that's how she got so much done.

Whatever it was, Lark stood behind her chair, her fingers tapping the back edge.

"Remember the three girls we had here over the winter?"

Mabel remembered well. Annabelle, Bernice, and Caren. They were sweet girls, seven, nine, and eleven years old. Too young for Lark to keep. Usually Lark had teenage girls and sometimes even girls who had graduated from high school but wanted to get their lives turned around.

Mabel had fallen in love with the young siblings and had taken them under her wing. She'd even given them her room, moving out to the couch so the girls had a place to stay.

"I loved them," Mabel said simply.

Lark nodded, a smile lifting her face. "I knew you did. And you were so good with them. They were...special."

"They were." Mabel touched the condensation on her tea glass, trying to ignore the pain that shot through her heart.

She figured out, sometime in the last ten years or so, that she had to open her heart to people, even though it was painful to lose them. She hated that pain and as a teenager held herself aloof from people in order that she wouldn't get so close to them, only to end up losing them.

Ironic that she lost her parents, which should have reinforced that desire, the desire to protect herself.

But that had really been the catalyst that cracked her heart and made her realize that life was short, and she needed to make sure she showed her love and people knew she cared.

Whenever it was, the three girls had stolen her heart like no one else ever had. She cried embarrassingly hard when they'd left.

"The grandmother wants to send them back. She's too old to care for them."

Mabel's eyes lit up. Her mind started to whirl. Could she take them? Could she do it? She would make it work. She would figure something out. Even if she had to hire a nanny to keep them while she worked.

Lark didn't have a clinic, so pretty much everything they did was farm calls. Anything that needed to be done in a sterile, clinical environment, they sent to the college clinic in Boise.

So, it wasn't like she was gone for eight hours a day every day. She might be gone for twelve hours one day and then only two the next. Or she might have a day in the middle of the week off. She never knew.

"I'll do it. I'll take them." Mabel wasn't sure whether that was what Lark was asking or not, but she wanted to make sure that Lark knew she was eager, desperate maybe, to have the girls again. She wanted them to have the best opportunity possible to thrive, and they'd already been through so much, with their mother in jail and their father... No one knew exactly who or where their father was. Mabel wasn't even sure they all had the same father. But she never voiced that question aloud.

"I thought you would." Lark's hand gripped the back of the chair, then, as though she were forcing herself to relax, she pulled the chair out and settled herself in it.

She didn't touch the tea on the table in front of her.

"But she won't let us have them."

"What?" Mabel said, her thoughts coming to a screeching halt. "I thought you said—"

"The grandmother called me. She wants a home for them, but she doesn't want them to come here."

"Why not?" Mabel asked, and she could hear her voice rising.

"It's okay. It's nothing that we did, exactly. It's just what we are."

"What do you mean?"

"She wants the girls to have a father in their life. I... I understand that. And I think that's a good thing."

"Of course it's a good thing. Study after study has shown being in a home with a mom and a dad, married and stable, will help children thrive, but that's not the way the world works. Sometimes you just can't do what's best, and you have to do what you can."

"I know. I know." Lark's hand covered Mabel's, and Mabel felt some of her tension draining out. Lark was never still, always seemed to be busy, but she had more patience than anyone Mabel knew.

And she was completely unvengeful. Even if the grandmother had told her they were terrible people and she would never allow her grandchildren to set foot in their house again, Lark would be explaining why the grandmother was probably right, that she was allowed to have her own opinion, and they should just focus on what they could do, not get upset about what they couldn't.

Mabel had heard all of it more than once.

Lark had a way of making things make sense, and Mabel had watched as she worked her magic on many of the girls who had stayed with her.

"I... I have someone I could ask. I don't really want to get married. I..." Lark's voice trailed off, and she looked off into the distance.

Mabel could only imagine that she was thinking about the one man she had loved at one time and had never truly gotten over.

"I don't love this man, and I never will, but I think I could propose a marriage of convenience to him, and he would accept."

"Who?" That was not the most important question, but it was the one that tumbled off Mabel's lips.

"Do you remember Paul, from in town in Sweet Water?"

"Paul?" Mabel asked, her stomach tilting dangerously. Paul wasn't a terrible-looking man, but he just had a way about him that seemed kind of sneaky. There had been rumors, unsubstantiated, that he was addicted to porn. He worked in IT and spent a lot of time on his computer. Mabel had never given credence to rumors, but the way Paul looked at her when she met him on the street gave her the creeps. It wasn't a respectful, friendly look, it was...almost a leer.

"Would he be the best father for the girls?"

"I think that I could pay him to stay where he is, and I would stay where I am, but I would technically have a husband, which would meet the criteria that the grandmother has set down. She wants the girls to go to a married couple." Lark's lips pressed together, and she breathed out slowly.

Mabel wanted to protest. Lark had someone she loved. Mabel was sure of it. And if Lark married Paul, she would never get the chance to be with the person that she truly loved. Mabel didn't know if there was even a chance of that happening, but if there was, it would be ruined if Lark did what she was saying.

But she had to admit Lark was right. She could marry Paul, then pay him to stay where he was, and the girls would not be affected.

Lark had money. Mabel wasn't sure exactly where it came from, but she never seemed to lack.

That was a mystery for another time.

"I'll get married." She didn't know the words were going to come out of her mouth, didn't even know they were in her head, until they spilled out, tumbling across the table and falling to the floor while Mabel looked on in horror.

"You?" Lark asked, and despite the total disbelief and shock in her tone, Mabel did not take offense.

She didn't exactly have suitors lined up for blocks. She really had never had a boyfriend. She just hadn't been interested. She put her blinders on, and had decided what she wanted to do with her life, and hadn't taken them off to even look around to see if there was anyone who would be suitable for her.

"Yes, me. I'm the one who loves the girls. I want them. I'll—"

"I was hoping that you would help me with them. I wasn't thinking that I would take them from you, I just knew that there was no chance of you getting married. And the only solution I could come up with was me."

"I'll marry Paul. Instead of paying for a nanny, you and I can share responsibilities, and I'll pay Paul to stay away, the same way you would. Only I... I don't have anyone that I would rather be with."

"But you might."

"No." She said that with assurance. She had never found anyone she was the slightest bit interested in spending the rest of her life with. Her parents had not been happy in their marriage, and while Gladys seemed to be madly in love with Silas, even after having been married for years, Mabel didn't hold a lot of hope for herself. A marriage of convenience sounded like the perfect solution if she wanted the girls, and one that wouldn't be too hard, although even discussing the situation with Paul gave her the shivers.

"I can handle Paul, but..." Lark's voice trailed off.

"It's okay. I won't be offended. I know you're older than I am, wiser, and you're probably right. It would be easier for you to handle Paul than me. Plus, he's a good bit older than I am. My parents' age, actually. But for the girls, I'll do it."

"Maybe there's someone else?" Lark asked, and her words seemed almost gentle.

Mabel caught the new tone but didn't give it much thought as she ran the eligible men who lived in Sweet Water and the surrounding areas through her head. She had been on almost every ranch in the area at some point and knew almost all of the men, she was sure.

There weren't any that she could imagine walking up to and suggesting a marriage of convenience and having them say yes. Definitely none that she could say that they would just stay on their farm while she continued to be a vet, and it would be in name only.

All of them would want to get married to someone for real at some point.

She put her elbow on the table and dropped her cheek into her hand. "I can't think of anyone."

Lark sighed. "I'm coming up with a blank too. There are some eligible men, but none who would be happy with just a marriage of convenience."

"Same."

And then, as soon as she said that word, a picture of a box came into her head.

Lark knew all about her fascination with Annie Oakley and how she loved anything to do with the sharpshooting woman from the 1800s. But she hadn't told Lark about the box. About going home tonight and opening something that belonged to Annie Oakley at one point.

But as she was thinking that, a face shimmered across her brain.

James. Carol's nephew. He'd worked with her dad. He hung out in the big city. He...was a man of the world and had never married.

He never married.

She couldn't imagine that James had someone he was pining for and hadn't gone after her. He must be single by choice. Maybe he wanted to stay that way. Maybe being married in name only would be something he would be interested in.

Could she ask him?

Oh yeah. She could totally see herself marching up to him and laying it out for him. She would do it for the girls, even though it wasn't something that she necessarily wanted to do.

"I think I have someone."

Chapter 4

"It was good of you to come see me, uh, the truck so quickly," James said as he shook Silas's hand.

"I don't always get a lunch break, but things were a little slow in the shop, so I figured I would slip out. Is that her over there?" Silas asked, nodding at the barn and the truck that slumped beside it.

"That's her," James said, feeling a little weird discussing the truck like it had a gender but imitating Silas.

"You don't seem like the kind of man who's interested in restoring old vehicles. I was a little surprised to get your call today," Silas said as they strode over.

James could work people. He'd done it in his younger years, but he knew it left him feeling hollow and empty inside.

A lot of people felt triumph when they got their way no matter how it happened, even if they had to hoodwink people in order to get it. That wasn't the kind of man he was, and...as much as he would like to continue with the charade, he found himself unable to say anything but the truth.

"Well, I'm really not."

"Oh? A new hobby?" Silas asked as he continued to walk.

"Not really. It was an excuse."

"An excuse?" Silas asked, matching his stride to James, and when James stopped, Silas did too, shoving a hand in his pocket and looking at James underneath the brim of his cowboy hat.

"Yeah. I wanted to talk to you about something else, and I guess I used the truck because I couldn't actually come right out and tell you, because it's...not something that most people would think was normal."

"Well, if you haven't noticed, Sweet Water is full of people who aren't exactly normal."

"I think the world is full of people like that," James said, glad that Silas didn't seem upset. Although, he hadn't exactly admitted what was really on his mind.

"So what's up?" Silas asked. Then he glanced back over at the truck. "You're really not interested in fixing it up?"

"The idea is a nice one, but I would be lying if I said I knew anything or had any interest other than passing."

Silas jerked his head up and then seemed to drag his eyes away from the dilapidated old vehicle.

"It's about Mabel."

There. The words just came out. Forced, but out nonetheless.

"Gladys's sister, Mabel?" Silas's body shifted, like he was going on high alert. That was what James was afraid of. Silas felt protective of his wife's little sister. He was sure of it. And he appreciated it.

This wasn't exactly how he had seen himself having this conversation, but he plowed ahead.

"Yes. That Mabel. I... I'm interested in her. Have been for a while."

"I know."

That stopped James in his tracks. First Aunt Carol, now Silas.

"Does the rest of the world know too?" James couldn't help but say. "I thought I did a really good job of making sure that no one knew, and you're the second person today that told me that they knew."

"I knew the day you came to their house after her parents died. It was obvious to me, but I admired you for doing the right thing. She might not have been too young, but she had goals and dreams and plans, and if you had stepped in, you might have derailed her."

James didn't say anything for a moment, because he hadn't expected Silas to see all of that. But that's exactly what he had done.

He stepped back, because he knew Mabel had a lot of potential and had things that she would be really good at. Being a vet was one of those things, and he didn't want to keep her from being what she was born to be.

He just felt that he was born to be her husband.

"You're more astute than I gave you credit for," James finally murmured.

"I might be a gearhead, but I do have eyes. And I have a wife too, who might have noticed the same thing. But she hasn't said anything either. Not to Mabel. We... thought perhaps your feelings might have shifted over the years, since you haven't been around as much as I was expecting."

"I was busy building my business, but that wasn't very satisfying, even though it was more successful than I ever envisioned it would be."

"I see. Sometimes we chase after things when it's really God who satisfies."

That hadn't been the way James's thoughts were going, but Silas was probably right. But if he had been born to be Mabel's husband, then God was manipulating things so that was the way they would end up. He might want to spend a little more time thinking on that, later. For now, he shoved the thought aside.

"Mabel doesn't seem to know I exist. I've never seen any spark of interest in her eyes at all, and I... I know she's special. Different. In the best way. It's part of her allure, and I just don't know how to approach her."

"The same way you'd approach any woman," Silas said offhandedly.

"I don't usually approach women. My aunt said I was charming, and I suppose that's true, but since I saw Mabel, man, it's been years, I haven't made any effort to be in a relationship with anyone else."

Silas grinned a little. "That's what I was hoping to hear."

"I know. It's weird. And normal people don't do that, but... There's just something about her, and no other woman compares. I just can't get interested in anyone else."

He quit trying to explain it, because he couldn't explain it to himself. There had been more than one time over the years where he wondered if he was even normal.

"You don't have to say anything more. I appreciate hearing what you said." Silas was quiet for a bit, as though he were thinking. "I'm a terrible person to ask about this. My wife is much better. Obviously she knows her sister better for one, and she knows all the romantic things that women want, while I have a tendency to get a little bit more enraptured with trucks." He smiled sheepishly, and James totally understood.

Women were much better at the romance things, but it seemed like men were the ones who were expected to do the romance things. It hardly seemed fair.

"I'm all ears for any advice. I... I really have no idea of how to proceed."

"Mabel's pretty self-contained. She isn't very emotional, and she doesn't talk much. I couldn't tell you what kind of man she would like, because I've never seen her with one. But you seem to be compatible with her, where you're a little bit more talkative, and she's a little less. But maybe she wants someone who will sit quietly beside her. I really don't know."

"I can be quiet if I need to be."

"Well, I think that's a bad idea." Silas shrugged a shoulder. "You can do whatever you want to, but I don't think that you want to try to be someone you're not. That's really not fair to her and is not fair to you either."

"I know. I just want to catch her eye."

"She seems like someone who's in it for the long haul. I guess I wouldn't think that you're going to catch her eyes so much as you're just going to slowly wear her down. I wouldn't pass up any opportunities to be around her, but I would try not to be overbearing, I guess." Silas shook his head. "The only thing I've really seen her passionate about are the three girls that she had over this past winter. They were the light of her life. I've never seen her smile so much and laugh too."

James tried not to be jealous. He wanted to be the one to make her smile and laugh, but it was silly to be jealous of three little girls. He tucked the information away. Mabel loved children.

"I'm not sure exactly on the specifics, but they went home I think to their grandma. Regardless, she loves animals, she loves children, and she is fiercely loyal. If you win her, you'll have her for the rest of your life. That much I can guarantee."

James nodded. He already knew that. It was one of the things he loved about her. Her dad hadn't been much of a dad, but Mabel had loved him and had been on his side, supporting him no matter what. She might have been reading a book in the corner, but if there was a discussion at the table, and she was following it, her dad was the one she was rooting for.

"It's too bad about the truck," Silas mused, taking another glance at it.

"You know, it might be a little bit romantic to fix up an old truck and drive around together. If you're interested, and you think you can do it, I'll pay you for it."

"It would almost be an honor to fix it, and I'd only charge you for parts. Mind if I take a look?"

Silas moseyed over, and James walked beside him. They talked about the truck a bit, with Silas thinking that he might not be able to do all original parts, but he would be able to make it look like an original.

James found himself interested despite himself, but the idea of Mabel was not far from his mind. He was trying to put together a game plan based on what Silas had said.

Find some kid somewhere, get some animals, and hope she noticed him.

It didn't seem like much to go on.

After about fifteen minutes, he and Silas came to an agreement, with Silas saying that he would be back after work that evening with his rollback to haul the truck to his home shop.

"I can see if Gladys will put in a good word for you. I can do that myself, but I'm sorry I can't come up with anything better."

"That's not your fault. And I would definitely appreciate that."

James appreciated anything that would help him, although there was a part of him that acknowledged that maybe Mabel would never be his. He had to be okay with that.

Silas was just pulling away when a cloud of dust appeared that followed a car down the driveway.

It was Mabel's SUV, and she was traveling a little bit faster than normal.

James's stomach growled, but he ignored it. Instead, he felt like he needed to grab something and start running to help, although he wasn't sure what he should grab and what he was helping with. It was just the idea that Mabel was obviously concerned about something.

She didn't even stop to talk to Silas, but waved at him, and then kept flying toward the house.

The brake lights came on in Silas's truck, and James thought he might be turning around, but he didn't and disappeared in the distance as Mabel's car screeched to a short stop, gravel flying, at the front of the house.

He found himself jogging toward her door, although she had it open and was standing beside it by the time he got there.

"James," she said his name breathlessly.

"Yeah?" He found himself holding his breath. It was like she had come in such a rush just to talk to him.

"I need to talk to you."

It was. It was because of him.

"What's wrong?"

"Nothing. Nothing's wrong. I just... I need to talk to you."

She stepped out from behind her door and closed it.

He noticed that she was slightly cleaner than she had been when she left a few hours ago.

"All right. Where do you want to talk?"

Before she could answer, Aunt Carol stuck her head out the door. "Are you here for lunch? Because it's ready."

James's stomach growled in response, and Mabel, who seemed rather preoccupied, glanced at it and stared for several moments before it seemed to dawn on her that he was hungry.

"We can eat first. Sounds like you need to." She said that with a little bit of humor in her voice, but her lips only quirked a little, like her whole mind was focused on what she wanted to talk to him about.

"Food can wait if this is urgent."

"It is not. And normally I go about things in a slightly more disciplined way, but... This is important to me, and... I probably should have spent a little more time thinking before I came running to you."

"You can run to me anytime," he said and hoped it didn't sound too sappy. He didn't want to say things just for the sake of saying things, and he didn't want her to think he was the kind of man who did that.

Words like that were meaningless, especially if he said the same thing to every woman he met.

Which he didn't, but Mabel wouldn't know that. Not now. And she might not believe him if he started spouting off all the pretty words he wanted to say to her.

Somehow thinking of the pretty words reminded him of the box his aunt had been talking about but hadn't seemed to want to tell him about.

"All right. Let's go eat first, and then maybe we can sit on the front porch. I have a proposition to make."

"Don't forget about the box. We definitely want to know what's in the box too."

"Oh my goodness. I totally forgot about that too." Mabel shook her head. "Today has been quite a day, and it's only lunchtime."

They walked into the house, with James holding the door while Mabel murmured thank you and stepped in.

James realized he hadn't even made it into the house since he'd arrived. He'd spent so much time outside, first with Mabel, then Silas, and he hadn't had breakfast that morning.

Part of him was dying to know what Mabel wanted to say, and part of him was just happy to go in and sit down, eat, and have a little time to spend with her.

Silas was most likely right. She wasn't going to be swept off her feet; she was far too practical for that. She needed someone she knew was going to be there for her for the long haul. Someone who depended on God and would lead his family that way. Someone who had always been in her corner. Someone whose loyalty she would never question. Someone who showed her with his actions that she was the most important thing to him.

It could take years.

James was prepared to do whatever it took, for however long it took.

"I remembered that you loved my lasagna growing up, and I've made it for Mabel once, and she enjoyed it as well. So, that's what we're having." Aunt Carol bustled around the kitchen. The table was already set, but she pulled garlic bread out of the oven while Mabel put an oven mitt on the table and set the lasagna down on top of it.

Knowing that Aunt Carol always had sweet tea in the refrigerator, James went to the refrigerator and pulled the container out.

"Would you like tea?" he asked Mabel, remembering that back when she was with her father, she usually got water. Normally with a lemon. Funny the things he remembered.

It was also kind of sad considering that she had been young, and he shouldn't have even noticed her.

Still, he had not acted improperly with her at all, and even now, he would keep in mind that she always had the right to say no, and he would accept it.

He might not like it, but he would accept it.

"Yes please," she answered as she grabbed the spatula from the drawer and brought it to the table.

They all sat down, and Aunt Carol looked at him to say grace.

It was something he had done for every meal he'd eaten at Aunt Carol's house since his mother had died, but he felt a little shot of nervousness go through him now that Mabel was sitting at the table too.

But Silas's words rang in his ear. He was not going to try to be someone he wasn't. He would just be who he was, and if that was good enough for Mabel, then that was right.

So, he bowed his head and said a simple prayer. He had never been the kind of person who said big, long prayers while the food was growing cold.

He'd save those for the devotion time he had every evening before he went to bed.

He said amen, and Aunt Carol spoke immediately.

"James, would you dish the lasagna for us?"

"Sure," he said and reached for the spatula.

He gave some to Aunt Carol first, and then to Mabel, and then dished himself last. Very aware the entire time of Mabel watching.

He wished he could read her thoughts, know what she was thinking of all this. Of whether he was doing it right or not, but then he reminded himself again of Silas's words.

Just be yourself.

That eased his nervousness somewhat, and he said, "I've been curious about the box. I hope that I get to be around when you guys open it. You said it was from Annie Oakley?"

"That's what I heard. I brought it with me from Oklahoma. There was a friend of mine who wanted me to pass it along to someone who...loved Annie and who could use it. I thought of Mabel, not long after I moved here and she talked about moving in with me. She has a great heart, and I know she loves Annie Oakley."

"I used to try to figure out how I could make a living with something that had to do with Annie. I suppose I could start a museum, but that didn't seem like a very profitable venture. And I like to eat almost as well as I like Annie Oakley."

They laughed around the table, and James forgot his nervousness as they talked about some of the facts of the great sharpshooter, things he hadn't known. Annie had never been someone on his radar. He wasn't exactly brought up to be a lover of the Old West. New technology, new business innovations, and always trying to figure out how to work people to his advantage were the things that his dad had tried to teach him.

Spending time with Aunt Carol had been a relief from all that pressure, but he still hadn't gotten interested in the Old West.

Still, as Mabel discussed some of the facts of Annie's life, he found himself intrigued. He also wondered what kind of artifact would be in the box.

He supposed he would find out soon enough.

Chapter 5

Mabel couldn't believe she had almost jumped out of her car and asked a complete stranger to marry her with no warning whatsoever.

She was grateful that Carol had come out of the house and called them to dinner.

It was much better to break the ice, so to speak, as they ate and talked about Annie Oakley, and the box, and of course she had to say how delicious the lasagna was.

James was actually funny, and she appreciated the fact that he held doors and wasn't afraid to pray. That surprised her, since she saw him as a city guy who was too modern for any of the things she might consider important.

He had been a colleague of her dad's, but she didn't really remember anything else about him. Some of her dad's colleagues had been more crooked than straight.

None of them had kept in touch after his death.

Still, James didn't really talk about his business at all but seemed interested in the fact she was interested in Annie, and he also complimented his aunt several times on the lasagna.

As they finished their meal, she got up with her plate and carried it to the sink, setting it down and turning, only to find him standing behind her with the pan of lasagna.

"Oh. I'm sorry. Excuse me," she said. She hadn't expected him to get up and help.

"Sure. It was my fault for standing too close." He set the pan of lasagna on the oven and then pulled out a drawer, getting some aluminum foil to put over the top.

"You seem very comfortable here," she commented as she grabbed a rag to wipe the table.

"I grew up with Aunt Carol. She didn't exactly raise me after my mother died, but I spent a lot of summers at her house, most holidays, and more than a few weekends."

"And I loved every second of it. He was the perfect child, and I would have kept him all the time if his father would have allowed it."

"Dad would have let you, if he hadn't been so set on me learning the business. The older I got, the less he wanted me to come see you, and the more I wanted to."

"You mean you didn't want to go into business? But you did it because of your dad?"

"I had to do something to make a living," James said casually as he ripped off the aluminum foil and fitted it carefully over the top of the lasagna. "That seems to be what I was groomed for, and I can't say that I resisted, especially once I was out of high school and started in college. I...wanted to do something that I could make a living at, and that seemed to be presented right in front of me. I didn't buck it too hard."

"That wasn't your interest?"

"I guess not. I...didn't really have an interest." His voice was a little soft, like maybe he did have an interest, but either it was personal or he wasn't sure about what it was. Maybe he didn't want to talk badly about his dad, who had pushed him in a different direction.

"I guess I was lucky that way. I've always wanted to be a vet, and things just worked out that I was able to. After my parents died, I wasn't sure whether I would have the money to go to college or not, but somehow it just was always there." She finished wiping the table and straightened. "I didn't realize you lost your mother."

"Yeah, I think I was ten. It was hard, but you get over it." He brushed it aside, and she couldn't blame him. Sometimes she didn't want to talk about the death of her parents. They hadn't exactly been a family who had been super close, but losing one's parents was always hard. She couldn't imagine a little boy losing his mother. At least she had been older.

Mabel hadn't considered asking James to be anything more than a husband in name only. Someone who would marry her, then forget he had a wife when he returned to the big city. She had thought he wouldn't be interested in anything more, and she had certainly not been.

But then, he had surprised her with his conversation at the table, and part of her felt that maybe she was asking the wrong person. Maybe there was more to him than the desire to make his business as big and successful as it could possibly be. Maybe he really would be interested in having a wife and family.

She had been using the standard she'd used for her dad, who had very seldom been around the family, and the only time she really saw him was when they went on business trips together. And that she felt was more because she was socially awkward, and he thought somehow getting her around his business associates would loosen her up, or make her talk, or whatever it was he thought.

Most of the time, she thought he was embarrassed by her, even though she couldn't stop herself from defending him and being on his side anytime there was a discussion that she had no choice but to be involved in.

Most of the time, she chose to read in a corner, but if she was sitting at a table with his business associates, whatever she did she supported her dad.

It just seemed to be the way families should operate, even if it didn't always seem like it was the way her family operated.

Maybe it was her conscience saying she misjudged James, or maybe she shouldn't have judged him at all. Or that she was using him.

That didn't sit right with her, and she shoved that thought aside as hard as she could.

"How about you go out on the porch, I'll grab the box, and we'll open it together." Carol spoke as she finished up the last of the dishes, and Mabel took it from her, drying the dish carefully before she put it in the cupboard.

"That sounds good to me. I can't wait to see what's in it!" she said, the thoughts of marriage and the three girls somehow settling a little further from her brain.

She really did love everything about Annie Oakley, and she couldn't wait to see what the box held. And there was a part of her that was feeling worse and worse about her decision to proposition James and didn't mind procrastinating.

They walked through the house, with James holding the front door open while she stepped outside. It was a beautiful sunny day, with a bright blue sky, puffy white clouds, and North Dakota grasses stretching in all directions.

"This house is so close to town, yet so private. I just love it. I didn't even realize it was here most of the time I've lived here," she murmured as she walked to the banister and leaned against it.

James came over and stood beside her, a good two feet between them but his hands also leaning on the banister as he looked over the waving grasses. "I fell in love with it the moment I saw it. And I have to admit that it was not nearly as nice then as it is now."

"You've owned it for years?" She couldn't keep the surprise out of her voice.

"Yeah. I don't even know how many...ten maybe? I just... It's so big and beautiful, so welcoming. And I guess maybe I thought someday I'd have a farm. Not that I know anything about farming."

He laughed, a little self-effacing laugh. "I certainly don't look like a farmer."

She couldn't deny that, with his soft white hands and his shiny leather shoes.

He wore some kind of shirt that looked expensive, and although the top button was unbuttoned, it looked like it could go with a tie without too much trouble.

His khaki pants went nicely with the deep blue of his shirt, and it brought out the deep blue of his eyes. She found herself happy that he wasn't wearing a cowboy hat, which would have shaded his eyes and made it harder to see the pretty color.

What a silly thought.

She pulled her eyes away and looked back toward the barn. What was she thinking? She didn't care about his eyes. She didn't care about anyone's eyes.

"I hadn't known that. So did you renovate a lot of it?" She asked the first question that came to her mind.

"From top to bottom pretty much. I even put a foundation under it, since it didn't have one, just a crawl space. That was probably the biggest change I made. That, and when I took the old windows out and replaced them with new, I made them bigger. That was a rather large expense, but the house was already so bright and cheerful, I thought bigger windows, while they aren't economically smart, just seemed a lot nicer than small ones that keep the house dark."

"I love the big windows. That's probably my favorite thing about the house, other than the high ceilings, which again, probably make it very difficult to keep heated in the winter."

"And the fall and spring, which are also cold here in North Dakota."

"That's true."

He seemed like he was going to ask another question, but Carol walked out on the porch just then carrying the box, and he turned toward her.

"That looks expensive," he murmured.

"And old," Mabel added, walking beside him to reach Carol.

"It definitely makes it seem like whatever's inside could be old and expensive," Carol said with a smile.

"You want to sit down?" Mabel asked, knowing that Carol's legs hurt if she was on them too long, and she'd already cooked lunch.

"Don't mind if I do," she said, walking over to the swing and settling down on it.

He jerked his chin and gave a wave with his hand, and she took that to mean that he wanted her to sit.

He moved to the banister, leaning against the post and crossing his arms over his chest, his face holding interest but giving them space.

She turned back to Carol who ran her finger over the top of the box.

She seemed to be stalling, and Mabel could understand why. Now that the moment was here, she wanted to drag it out a little too. Make it last. It was special, a once-in-a-lifetime thing, and she didn't want it to be over too soon.

Still, she was dying to know what was in the box.

"Are you ready?" Carol asked quietly.

"I am. I think." She laughed nervously.

Carol nodded. She carefully undid the clasp and opened the box.

Mabel wasn't sure what to think. Nestled in the deep velvet folds was an old-looking pistol.

A gun.

She hadn't anticipated seeing a gun. Of course, Annie Oakley was known as the most famous sharpshooter of the Old West, but still. A gun?

"Can I say I am a little disappointed?" Mabel said slowly.

As much as she admired Annie, it was more because of how she had learned about how Annie had supported women. How she had forged a path in a mostly male-dominated world, how she had gone forward but held out a hand behind her, helping those to come along, giving them a hand. Giving them confidence in themselves, and caring about her fellow humans.

It wasn't really because of the guns.

In fact, that was probably the one thing that she and Annie definitely did not have in common.

Mabel couldn't say for sure that she'd ever actually held a gun before.

"It's beautiful," Carol breathed. "I don't think I've ever seen anything quite like it before. It's...pink."

"That's what I was thinking. So odd, the pink handle. It's...not a gun handle I've ever seen before. Is that what it's called? The handle?"

"I don't know. I don't know anything about guns." Carol almost seemed dismissive. "Here. You have to be the one to take it out."

"I have to be the one? What do you mean by that?"

Carol clamped her mouth shut, almost as though she felt like she had said too much.

It made Mabel curious. What was Carol saying?

But she held the case over so that it was right in front of Mabel, and Mabel felt like she probably didn't have a choice. She carefully reached out and slowly stroked one finger down the handle of the pistol before she wrapped her fingers around it and lifted it from the box.

It felt heavy in her hand. Although, having never held a gun before, she wasn't sure whether that was normal or unusual.

"It seems fitting that a gun from Annie would look feminine." James's words caused Mabel to jerk. She'd forgotten that he was there.

She wasn't sure exactly what she did, although she knew she almost dropped the gun, and as she grabbed for it with her other hand, she felt something click underneath her, and knowing the one rule of gun safety was to never point it at anything one didn't intend to shoot, she was careful as she was fumbling for the gun to keep it pointed away from her.

Therefore, when the gun went off, she did not shoot herself.

She shot James instead.

Chapter 6

Well, that was awkward.

Mabel dropped the gun back in the case and said abruptly, "Close it!"

Jumping to her feet, she clasped her hand over her mouth as blood slowly stained the porch floor beside James's feet.

Any thought she had that the man might actually be willing to marry her was shot.

Ugh. Terrible pun.

Mabel castigated herself for having that be her first thought. Her first thought should have been for his safety. But thankfully, it was his foot that seemed to have borne the brunt of her ineptitude. Thankfully.

"I am so sorry. I could have killed you. I should have known better than to touch it."

She flew over and knelt down by his foot, her medical training coming to the forefront.

"I happen to know someone who is able to do stitches and can numb that up for you. I think it might be just a surface wound. Although, I'd really like to remove your shoe and sock and check it out. If you'll let me?"

"I guess there are advantages to being shot by a vet," James deadpanned.

She looked up at him. He didn't seem angry. "Aren't you going to yell at me?"

"Why?"

"Because I was careless. And stupid. And I shot you!" She said that last bit a little louder, because *she had shot a man.*

"But it was an accident." He limped over and sat down on the step.

"I'm sorry. You could have the swing." Carol made as if to stand.

"Actually, it's probably better for him to sit here. The steadier he is, the better." Mabel removed his shoe as she spoke, and her heart pinched as he flinched at the pain.

She carefully pulled his sock down and slid that off as well.

How could she have shot the man she was hoping to ask to marry her? She had to be the most romantically challenged woman in the entire world.

Thankfully, as she pulled his sock off, she realized that the bullet hadn't lodged in his foot, which she had to admit she was grateful for, since she didn't have any experience in removing bullets from animals nor people.

Or porches. She glanced behind her. It was probably stuck in the wood somewhere. They could worry about that later, but it was one more mark against her. She'd ruined his porch floor in a way she never thought she would.

"I guess I didn't give you the option to go to the emergency room. You can do that if you want to." She didn't usually take over like she just had and insist on using her medical skills on people.

Of course, she didn't typically shoot people either.

This was all very new to her.

"I don't enjoy hanging out in hospitals, so if you can take care of me here, that would be ideal."

"Let me go get my bag. I have some things that will clean this up, and you might need a couple of stitches, but it's actually looking a lot better than what I had been afraid it would."

The bullet hadn't gone deep at all, and honestly, she didn't even think it really needed stitches.

"The hardest thing with a foot is making sure it doesn't get infected. So my recommendation would be to stay off of it for a while, especially if I put a few stitches in it."

"All right. I wasn't sure how long I was going to hang with Aunt Carol, but I'll just rearrange my schedule in Chicago and make sure that it's long enough to recover."

She nodded. She was suddenly feeling a little shy, although she wasn't sure whether it was because she shot him, or whether it was because of the way he was looking at her.

It seemed almost...personal. She could hardly explain, but it made her heart shiver and her backbone curl.

She stumbled a bit as she stood, grabbing the door and hurrying inside.

She thought she heard Carol chuckling behind her, but maybe that was just her imagination. Heading to the mudroom on the other end of the house, where she kept her spare medical supplies, she grabbed her extra bag, which contained everything she would need, and ran back through the house, trying to think of what else she should do. Normally, she wouldn't work on a human. It was actually illegal, but considering that she shot him... She hadn't even thought about it. He could press charges. He could have her jailed.

Her eyes got wide. Surely he wouldn't do that.

Of course, it was an accident, and Carol would vouch for her. Although he was her nephew, and if Carol had to decide on who she was more loyal to, it would be her nephew and not the woman who had just moved into her house.

Taking a deep breath, she tried to calm herself as she opened the door and walked back out to the porch.

Whatever happened, she would have to face it.

Chapter 7

"So, Aunt Carol, I'm pretty sure that when a woman shoots a man, that's a sure sign that she's not interested in anything romantic."

James couldn't help but say that to his aunt as soon as he was sure Mabel was out of earshot.

Aunt Carol laughed. "It was an accident. I don't think you can read anything into it other than the woman should not be within five feet of the gun and preferably more." She shook her head and muttered, "And I had such high hopes for this."

"High hopes for what?" James asked.

"Oh, it's just that the pistol... I heard some things about it, and I knew how interested Mabel was in Annie Oakley, and I was hoping that it would help the two of you finally get together."

"The pistol? Help us get together? What are you talking about?" This was the second time today that she had totally baffled and confused him.

"Oh, really nothing, just... Maybe I'll tell you some other time. I think I hear her coming back."

He gave his aunt a look that said he wasn't very happy with the way she was beating around the bush, and then the door burst open, and a rosy-cheeked Mabel strode sedately out.

He was pretty sure she was trying to force herself to remain calm, and he almost laughed. It wasn't every day that a person shot someone and had to calm themselves down afterward.

"You know, if you want to turn me in to the police, I totally understand."

James blinked. He hadn't considered it. "Why would I do that?"

"Because I shot you!" Mabel exclaimed.

"You didn't mean to."

"Involuntary manslaughter?"

"But I didn't die."

"Yet."

"Should I find another doctor?"

"No. I don't think I'm going to kill you, but I just figured that things really couldn't get any worse, unless of course you do end up dying, and with the way my luck has been lately..."

"I trust you. Go ahead and do whatever needs to be done, and then we'll talk about whatever it was you wanted to talk about."

Maybe Aunt Carol thought that was a hint, because at that point, she stood up, still carefully cradling the box. "I'm going to go ahead and take this inside. I... I think that maybe we need someone who knows a little bit of something about guns to make sure it's unloaded before we attempt to look at it again."

"That's a really good idea. Although, I don't care much anymore that it belonged to Annie Oakley. I'm not sure I ever want to see it again. I definitely am not going to ever trust myself to touch a gun again."

"Sometimes it's just a matter of getting to know something and understanding it, and then it stops being so scary."

"Are you actually saying that you think I ought to learn more about guns rather than swearing them off?" Mabel sounded incredulous.

"Sure. I mean, if someone fell into a lake and almost drowned, wouldn't it be wise for them to take swimming lessons rather than avoiding water for the rest of their life?"

"Well, I can understand why someone who almost drowned would want to avoid water. But I suppose you're right. It would be smarter to develop the skills so that one would no longer have to fear what almost killed them."

He nodded. "That's exactly right."

He winced as she put something cold on his foot. The bleeding had almost stopped, and he watched as she tilted her head.

"I'm debating about stitches. I feel like it's a no. But I still think you're going to need to stay off your foot for at least a week until it heals. You don't want it to get infected."

"All right. I'll stay off my foot for at least a week."

"That was easy," she said, sounding surprised.

"Did you think I was going to fight about it?"

"Well, I'm not a human doctor, and my patients typically are not able to be reasoned with, but it's usually a struggle to get anyone, or anything, to stay down for an entire week."

"If it means that my foot will heal up properly, that's what I'll do."

She nodded, looking up at him with her lips tilted. "Sometimes people are just not reasonable, but that seems like a reasonable thing to do."

She nodded again, but from the way she acted, it felt like she didn't think most people were reasonable.

He wasn't sure that was a point in his favor or not, and he tried to keep his mind thinking about it as she worked on his foot, to keep it off the pain.

He wasn't thinking that he was going to cry like a baby, but he did have to grit his teeth over a couple of exclamations.

But then she numbed it, and he didn't feel anything.

"I cheated a little," she said after a bit. "I'm pretty sure the doctor wouldn't do that, but since I inflicted the pain, and since I had the power to un-inflict it for a little bit, that's what I did. But I did it because I believed you when you said that you would stay off your foot for a while. And you'll definitely need to do it until you get the feeling back in it."

"I can do that, but I think since you're the one who shot me to begin with, you probably ought to be keeping me company now."

"That's a good point," she said. "And I can do that, as long as I don't get any calls. I'm not on call this weekend, but if Lark is out and something else comes in, I might have to go."

"All right. You're excused for work purposes only. But unless something comes up, you are required to sit and keep me entertained so I'm not tempted to start practicing for the dancing lessons that I'm going to take someday."

She laughed, knowing right away that he was joking. Although dancing lessons had never crossed his mind, he could be persuaded if the right person wanted to partner with him.

The right person being Mabel, of course.

"You said you had something you wanted to talk to me about?" he asked as he shifted his weight just slightly, stretching his bandaged foot out in front of him and resting his shoulders and head on the post behind him.

"I do. Did. But I think I've changed my mind. But let me throw this stuff away and I'll be back out to sit with you."

"Why did you change your mind?" he asked before she could disappear into the house.

"I shot you. I can hardly ask a favor now."

She disappeared inside the door before he could assure her that she absolutely could ask a favor. That he would do anything she wanted him to. Anything.

Maybe he should play hard to get a little bit. Maybe he could use this whole shooting thing to his advantage. Of course, he already had, because now he had several uninterrupted hours with her to sit with him and for him to...charm her? He had already decided that charm wouldn't work.

What could he do to convince her that he was a great guy and she should spend more time with him?

A couple of hours didn't seem like nearly long enough for him to get her to believe that, and he almost wished that the gunshot had been worse.

Of course, if they did end up together, what a story he would have to tell the grandchildren.

"I'm glad you're finding something to smile about," she said as she stepped back out on the porch. "This might help too, since I was just in the kitchen, and Carol must feel so terrible for you she's making brownie cheesecake, which she assured me was your favorite."

"It is. Boy, I must have looked sufficiently wounded in order for her to do that."

"I think she just likes to make you happy. It's obvious that she adores you," Mabel said, walking over to the swing and sitting down on it.

He had wanted to be able to sit on the swing with her, and he was tempted to get up and hobble over, but remembering his promise, he stayed where he was.

"So... If I have to go somewhere," he was thinking about the bathroom, "how I do that?"

"Ah," she said. "You mean if you have to use the restroom?" She lifted her shoulder, and he was happy he didn't have to spell it out to her. Although, she didn't seem particularly fazed about it, so he felt like he could have mentioned it with impunity. "I think you probably ought to get the person who's keeping you company to help you."

Why hadn't he thought of that? He wouldn't even have to ask. He could have just mentioned that he needed to and assumed that she would come over and he would have an excuse to put his arm around her.

Maybe that was too creepy.

But since she suggested it, he almost took advantage of it right away. Except he really didn't have to go.

That might make it awkward for whenever he did.

"All right. I'll keep that in mind. Now, just because you shot me doesn't mean that you can't ask me what you were going to ask me. You said it was a favor?"

She had come to ask him a favor? He couldn't imagine what in the world it would be... Unless she wanted money.

He clamped his mouth shut and looked away. Why hadn't he thought of that? Probably because he'd been so busy getting shot that he hadn't had the time.

He couldn't keep the disappointment from filling his chest, making it feel tight and empty.

He'd been so sure that Mabel was different. But she probably just needed a couple of hours to remember that he was supposed to be loaded before she came running back to see if he would loan her money. He was sure she had a ton of good causes she worked for, and of course, he would say yes to whatever she asked for, but he had been hoping that it had been something more personal. That Mabel had been different, and it wouldn't all be about money for her.

"Did you change your mind?" she asked softly.

"About what?"

"About wanting me to tell you what my favor was. You don't look very happy."

"No. Go ahead. How much do you need?"

She blinked. Then her brows drew down, and her nose wrinkled.

"What?" she asked, as though she were trying to figure out what in the world he meant.

"Money. How much money do you need?"

"Oh my goodness. You thought I was going to ask you for money?" Then she laughed. "Oh, James. Wait till you hear what I actually am going to ask you. You'll wish that I would have been asking you for money."

It was his turn to be confused. She didn't want money? And she was laughing at him. Why was she laughing at him?

"So...I'm wrong?"

"Oh, you are so far off it's not even funny. I want so much more than money from you."

The weight in his chest started to drain out. She wanted more than money? What in the world?

"Okay. Now I'm intrigued. What is it?"

"All right. I'm just going to be straight with you. Last winter, I had the pleasure of mothering three young girls. But their mother is in prison, and no one is sure who their father is, if they even have a common father. They really need stability in their lives. I fell in love with them."

Silas had told him as much, but hearing it come from Mabel herself made his heart ache for her. It was obvious how much she cared about those children.

Whatever she wanted, he'd do it. Gladly. But he couldn't work magic. He couldn't bring the kids back to her. If that's what she even wanted.

"So, today Lark told me that their grandmother was in contact with her again and is looking for a home for them."

"That's awesome. I'm sure you volunteered. If you're going to ask if they can stay here—of course! When are they coming?"

"That's just it. She wasn't thinking of us. She liked them staying with us, but because they've had such an unstable life, and because there haven't been any good male figures in their lives, any of them, since their mother isn't married, and their grandmother doesn't have a husband either, their grandmother is insisting that they go to a home with a mom and a dad."

She emphasized "dad," and then she pushed a little with her foot and the swing creaked.

He was totally confused, having absolutely no idea where she might be going with this. So he waited. He could hardly buy a dad. He couldn't snap his fingers and provide one either. Maybe she knew one of his friends and she wanted him to ask one of his friends if they would provide a home for the girls. He tried to think of his buddies that were married, trying to figure out which one might be the best to provide the best home for the girls. Most of the couples he knew worked constantly, and the dads would hardly ever be home.

The mothers worked in those families too, and the girls would end up in daycare over the summer. He wasn't even sure that they might not go to daycare after school most days.

He couldn't think of a single one that he would highly recommend, although he had several he thought would be okay parents.

"I really want the girls," Mabel said, lifting her head and looking him straight in the eye. Her gaze pierced to his very soul, and he could tell that this was one of the most important things in the world to her. "I need a husband."

He hardly thought he heard right. But he didn't have a chance to ask her to repeat herself, because then she said, "And I want him to be you."

Chapter 8

James tried to swallow, but he couldn't get his dry mouth to provide enough spit to wet his throat.

Mabel, the woman that he'd been admiring for most of his life, had just...asked him to marry her.

Well, it was a weird marriage proposal as marriage proposals went, but still, it boiled down to the basics—she wanted to marry him.

He wanted to jump up and down, grab her and swing her around, and do the dancing that he had been joking about earlier.

Just in time, he remembered his foot. He couldn't feel it, but he knew he had promised to stay off it.

"You want me to marry you?" he managed to say, and he thought his voice sounded almost normal.

"I did. It's crazy. But Lark had mentioned a marriage of convenience. Basically, you would marry me, so that I could say I had a husband, so that the grandmother will let me have the girls. You don't have to be a husband or a dad. You can stay in Chicago and never even notice that you have a wife and kids. I assume that you're not interested in getting married since you're so old and haven't found anyone, and I didn't have a chance to talk to Carol about it, but I was going to ask her and I thought that maybe this would all be just fine for you and I promise that I won't be a clingy or nagging wife; in fact, you don't even have to think of me as your wife, and if it's necessary for you, we could actually have the marriage annulled, although I hate making vows that I have no intention of keeping, so that doesn't sit very well with m—"

He put his hand up and said, "Hold on."

Her mouth clamped closed immediately.

She had called him old. He was still trying to get past that. Is that what she thought of him?

He had never seen Mabel ramble on like that. Normally while she seemed happy and easygoing, she didn't talk much at all. So that was new.

And now she had just said the very best and the very worst things that she could say to him.

How could she say both in one breath?

She'd asked him to marry her.

Then she told him that she didn't want to have a real marriage and that she didn't even want to see him. And that he was old.

Tempted to accept and give her any conditions she wanted—after all, marriage to Mabel had been his dream for as long as he could remember—he also knew that his dream had not included her sending him off to Chicago while she lived in North Dakota, and they never met again.

"I'm not against marrying you," he said slowly. Her eyes brightened, but concern lay like a thundercloud over top of them.

"But?" she prompted him.

"But I don't think marriage should be me living in Chicago and you living in North Dakota."

He let his words lie there while she seemed to chew on them. She bit her lip and looked away, gazing out the other end of the porch, at the waving grasses and the waning afternoon sun.

"All right. What do you suggest?" she asked, sounding almost hesitant, like she was afraid he was going to say that marriage wasn't a good idea after all.

"I understand how much those little girls mean to you. I've heard how much you love them, and it sounds to me like they desperately need a family. Two people who are willing to put the lives that they are raising first and nurture them as much as possible. I... I also agree with the grandmother. Children should have a mom and dad. Having a marriage of convenience where we live in different states really isn't the best thing for the kids, is it?"

She shook her head slowly, as though she had just thought of that.

"I didn't think that you would want to actually be married," she said, sounding unsure as she squinted her eyes and looked at him.

He didn't say anything for a few minutes, trying to figure out how he should word it. How he should say that he wanted to be married, live in the same house, raise a family together, be in love, love each other, and show it.

But he thought that might be a little bit overwhelming for her. And she might not be interested if she thought he was...old.

So, he settled down, trying to think. "I'll admit that I really hadn't been planning on getting married anytime soon." He took a breath and continued before she could interrupt him. "That doesn't mean that I have anything against being married, it just means that...I haven't found the right woman yet."

He hoped that sounded sufficiently competent. He knew that people could look at his dating history, or lack of it, and see someone who was a loser. Someone who wasn't "man enough" to attract a woman. But that really wasn't it at all. He just knew who he wanted and knew she wasn't ready to have him.

Now that she was, that she actually asked him, he wanted to manipulate the situation so that they didn't go their separate ways after saying the vows that would unite them for life.

He didn't mean to use the word manipulate. Because that made it sound like he was doing it in a selfish way, and maybe he was to some extent. But he knew what he was saying was true. The girls would be better off with a father in the picture, in the home, interested in them.

And he wanted Mabel.

Maybe, just maybe, Mabel would be more happy with him in the home than she would be without him.

"Do you really think I'm old?" he asked and was pleased to hear that his voice only sounded mildly curious and not hurt or scared. Scared that she looked at him and saw a father figure—not just for her kids, but for herself, too. He was only ten or so years older than she. Not enough to be anywhere near a father figure to her.

But she might not see it that way.

"No." She tilted her head. "What made you think that?"

"You said something about me being old and not being married." He was sure he heard it.

"Oh. I just meant that you were old enough to be married if you wanted to be. I thought maybe you'd chosen to be single."

"Oh." The relief that he felt did not come out in that word, but his whole body felt so light he was surprised he wasn't floating.

Back to the other issues.

"Do you want to be a single mom?"

"No?" she said, sounding like she had never thought of such a thing. "I just... I just don't have anyone lined up. I can't imagine even if I did put my mind to trying to find someone... I'm just not the kind of girl that men flock to."

"What makes you say that?" he asked, even though it really wasn't pertinent information to their conversation. He certainly would flock to her. It was odd to him that she wouldn't see her value, see how attractive he felt she was, and how much effort he had put in over the years to stay away from her so that she could finish her schooling and fulfill her dreams.

Maybe he should have spent less time trying to stay away and more time letting her know that he thought she was exactly the kind of woman that attracted a man. At least a man like him.

"Well, look around. Do you see anyone beating the door down?" Her words were a little sarcastic, and they made him feel bad.

"I'm sure they'll be coming at any second," he said, but she saw right through those words, and he wished he wouldn't have said them.

She didn't quite roll her eyes, but he got the feeling she wanted to.

"All right. I see what you're saying, I guess. But that's not really what I see when I look at you."

"What do you see?"

He wanted to tell her all the things he saw, but this wasn't the time. The idea of getting married could be blown out of the water if she decided that he was a stalker and a creepy one at that.

"You're dedicated and strong, and you know what you want. You've gone after it. And the thing that I've always admired about you is your loyalty. First to your dad, then to Lark, and now to these girls. You're willing to enter a marriage of convenience just to make a home for them. That's pretty admirable and definitely something that appeals to me."

"I would be loyal to you if we were to get married."

"I know."

Something curled around those words, something warm and sweet. They seemed to shimmer in the air. He hadn't meant to say them like that, like instead of saying "I know" he had said "I love you."

She seemed to notice the difference in his tone too, and his heart beat loud in the silence between them.

"But if you were thinking about getting married to someone at some point, I don't want to stand in your way. And I don't want you to do something that could possibly mess up your future. A divorce doesn't exactly look good on a man's resume, not to a future spouse. Not that it's a terrible thing, it's just...not something that you want to show if you don't have to."

"If I got married, I would have absolutely no intention of getting divorced. I would mean it for life." He said those words firmly, allowing no room for argument. That was one thing he was absolutely firm on. He wasn't going to just dabble in marriage, doing it while it was convenient. No matter what they wanted to call it. Convenient marriage or no. If he got married, he would be serious about it, and he would expect his wife to be serious about it as well.

Mabel nodded, her face thoughtful. "What if you find someone else?"

"I won't be looking. I will refuse to look." But he wasn't the only one in question here, and he said, "What if you do?"

"I told you I would be loyal. Isn't that what that means?" Then she seemed to shake her head, realizing she had to answer his question. "When I get married, my loyalty will be to my husband, for the rest of my life."

He already knew that, but he liked hearing her say it, and the words settled deep and right into his bones.

They sat together, neither one of them speaking, as he rolled things over in his head. He wanted to hash it out, get the details straight, figure out what they were doing, but none of that seemed very romantic, and it seemed like this probably should be a romantic time, except he had never been very good at romance. Had never practiced saying the right words.

Maybe he should just say the real words.

"I want a real marriage. But I understand that might be something we have to grow into. I think that's fine, but I do think that if we're doing this for the kids, then we should definitely do it right for the kids. But... It's also about us. Because when the kids are grown, you and I will still be married. I'd like it to be a good marriage. A happy one. One full of love. Even if you never fall in love with me, that doesn't mean our house can't be a happy home."

"That was very inspiring. I... I haven't thought about all the details. I just knew I wanted to save these girls. Knew I wanted to have them near me so I could love them the way they deserve to be loved. But your vision is so much bigger, you're seeing the whole picture, not just the details that I had been staring at."

"The details are important, but you're right, I have a tendency to look at the big picture."

"And that's important too."

Her words were spoken firmly, like she was trying to make sure that she made a point to tell him that he was right, and he smiled.

She didn't need to, but he appreciated that she was already showing her loyalty by making sure she gave him his due.

"Do you have a timeline on the girls?"

"No. Lark didn't say anything more, because neither one of us could see a marriage happening anytime soon. But if you're one hundred percent sure, I will text her and tell her...that I found a husband." She smiled. "Can we joke about this?"

"I think we can. Go ahead, tell her you found a gullible sucker who isn't afraid to be the only man in the house with four women." His eyes widened. "I'll be the only man in a house of four women. Five if we're living with Aunt Carol. Maybe I better rethink this."

Her fingers froze on her phone, and she looked up to see the smile on his face. Once she read it and realized he was messing with her, she laughed. "You scared me."

"No. Don't let me scare you. I said I would do it, and I meant it. I'm not going back. The only way it's not going to happen is if you change your mind."

"That is not going to happen. I... I really want the girls, but you've risen to the occasion, and I believe you're going to be an amazing father, and I think you're going to be a good husband too. I just hope... I hope I can be a good wife. I haven't put much thought into being anything other than a veterinarian and to some extent a mom to the girls staying with Lark. I'm not sure I'm going to make a very good wife, and the more time I spend with you, the more I feel like you deserve one."

"We can hash out those details later. I want to be a good husband, and I don't have any more idea of how to do that than you have about being a good wife. So, how about we just agree to give ourselves grace while we try to figure out exactly what our roles are going to entail?"

"You come up with some really great ideas. Have I ever told you that?" They laughed together, and he felt like maybe he'd actually handled the situation as well as he possibly could have.

After all, he was going to marry Mabel.

Chapter 9

J ames twisted on the porch swing, trying to find a comfortable spot.

Sitting around all day while Mabel was around keeping him company was one thing, but she had gotten called out not long after she had texted Lark, and he had ended up spending the last few hours by himself, which was not nearly as pleasant as what it had been when Mabel was there.

Still, it was hard to keep the smile off his face.

After all those years of waiting, wondering if God was ever going to give him a lifetime love, the woman he admired from a distance, doing what his dad wanted, working hard in the business, and deliberately being ethical about it, even when it wasn't a popular decision, or the most lucrative, his patience had finally paid off.

He spent a lot of the afternoon thanking God for this seismic shift that had happened in his life.

He certainly hadn't seen it coming. Of course, he had to get shot first, but that was a small price to pay, in his estimation anyway, to have Mabel propose marriage to him.

He shifted once more and thought about going in just to get a glass of water, thinking that surely Mabel wouldn't be upset with him if he did that much, when he noticed a vehicle coming down the lane.

The front porch faced the lane, and a person sitting on it could see almost the whole way to the state highway, which was just out of sight over the horizon.

It was perfectly private and beautifully serene, and he was so thankful he had bought it and seen the potential all those years ago.

As the truck came closer, he noticed it was a rollback. He had totally forgotten about Silas.

He chuckled a little to himself at trying to figure out what Silas's reaction was going to be when he told him that his advice had worked pretty well, so well in fact that he would be getting married...

He didn't even know when. That was something they hadn't talked about.

But he was actually living in the same house as Mabel, and he would be here when she got back from her call, so they could talk about it then.

Silas pulled around the side of the house, and he heard the door slam.

He thought he saw a second head in the passenger seat and wondered who Silas had brought. Maybe Gladys. She was going to be disappointed that her sister wasn't there.

But when Silas walked around the corner of the porch, he had a little boy, maybe five or six years old, striding beside him.

"Hey there, what happened?" Silas asked immediately, seeing his foot propped up on the swing with the gauze bandages around it.

"I got shot."

Silas's eyes flew from looking at his foot to searching his face. "I think you're serious."

"Dead serious," James said, and he didn't even crack a smile. He could have been dead. It was only by the grace of God that the bullet had gone to his foot.

"Well, I would be interested in hearing that story."

"I probably have a couple of stories you might be interested in hearing."

"Sure. We'd love to hear them." He put his hand on the head of the little boy who stood seriously beside him. "This is Timothy," he said, ruffling the boy's hair.

"Good to meet you there, kiddo. You come out to help your dad with that truck?"

"Yep. He said he needed someone, and I was just the man for the job."

James tried to keep a smile from spreading across his face. The little boy was just as serious as he could be.

"Mabel is here?" Silas asked, looking around.

"She was here, she shot me, then she left."

A long pause.

"She shot you?"

"Yep."

"Then I take it you didn't really take my advice." He grimaced. "Or my advice was just really, really bad."

"Oh, I took your advice all right. It worked pretty well, too."

"It did?" Silas asked, looking at the bandage on his foot again.

"Sure did. We're engaged."

Again, Silas's eyes flew from the bandages on James's foot to his face, searching it to see what in the world he was missing. "I think you're serious."

"I told you I had some stories for you. And I'm dead serious. About both. She shot me, and now she's going to marry me."

"If you guys have children, this is going to make a great story someday."

"I guarantee it. It's probably going to be my favorite one to tell too."

"All right, Timothy, think we have a few minutes to listen to this fella tell us what happened today? It might involve a gunfight."

"There was just one gun. And she had a hold of it. Not that I would have shot her if I had it."

"Oh, I'm sure you wouldn't have," Silas said, glancing at him.

Timothy nodded seriously, and Silas settled himself down on the top step, where James had been sitting when Mabel fixed his foot.

Timothy sat himself down beside his dad and lifted a leg up, draping a forearm over it, imitating his dad's position perfectly.

James proceeded to tell them the story of how he managed to get himself shot.

Silas laughed, shook his head, and laughed some more. "I don't know. Either you're the luckiest man alive, or God really thinks pretty highly of you."

"I know. He's given me everything I've ever wanted. I can't complain at all."

Just then, Aunt Carol came out, carrying three plates with cheesecake on them.

"I heard some male voices out here. Looks like Silas brought his best helper along. It's a good thing I just made brownie cheesecake," she said, going to Timothy first and offering him a plate.

Timothy lifted his eyes to his dad, his look eager.

Silas nodded, and Timothy took the plate. "Thank you, ma'am."

"You're welcome, sir. Anyone who's out helping his dad on a nice day like this instead of playing deserves a piece of brownie cheesecake."

Timothy smiled, big and wide, and then dug into his cheesecake.

Aunt Carol gave Silas a piece, then she walked over to the swing, handing James his. "How's the foot?"

"Starting to hurt. You're going to tell Mabel I stayed off it all afternoon while she was gone, right?"

"You know, I was going to tattle on you if you even so much as came into the kitchen for a taste of the batter, but because you didn't, I'll have a good report to give to your fiancée." Aunt Carol winked.

She'd sat out on the porch with James for a while after Mabel had left. He'd told her everything, or at least most of it, and she'd been tickled pink.

He hadn't realized him getting engaged would make Aunt Carol so happy.

But looking back, she had said something about the pistol helping him, and it had almost seemed a romantic type of thing, or something along those lines, and he wondered if she hadn't had something like this planned all along. Just, she hadn't had a chance to implement any of her plans, because the gun had gone off, and apparently Mabel had been planning on asking him to marry her all along.

It seemed like nothing had happened for years, and then everything descended at once pointing him toward Mabel.

Whatever it was, he wasn't complaining.

They ate their brownie cheesecake, Aunt Carol chatting with them for a bit before she went back inside, fanning her face and saying that it was getting awfully warm for a lady of her advanced years.

It wasn't even eighty degrees, but James supposed when a person lived in North Dakota, seventy felt downright balmy.

Silas chatted a bit about the things he wanted to do with the truck and asked for James's opinion. James had to admit that he knew less than nothing about trucks and would appreciate some guidance in the direction they should go.

Silas promised to send links later, showing him pictures and things that he had in mind. James promised to look at them, then Silas and Timothy knocked on the door, gave their plates to Aunt Carol, and walked around the house.

James could hear them working, but he told Silas that he'd promised Mabel he wasn't moving, and he was going to do everything he could to keep his promise. Not just because it was Mabel, although that did add a new dimension to things, but because he always tried to honor his promises. There had been a few times in his life when he'd been forced to break a promise, and he'd hated every second of that. The experience had made him more cautious, and he tried hard not to make promises he couldn't keep.

Just before Silas and Timothy left with the old Ford on the rollback, James watched as Billy moseyed across the front yard.

He'd completely forgotten about Billy.

Billy was supposed to be a matchmaking steer, but he hadn't thought... Surely not. It couldn't be Billy, couldn't be the gun, it had to be things that had been set in motion years prior, at least since last winter, when Mabel had fallen in love with the girls.

The fact that he was engaged to the girl of his dreams couldn't have anything to do with any other type of manipulation.

Right?

Chapter 10

Mabel finished tacking the stomach into place, snapped her suture, and then worked on clamping the cow's hide together so she could stitch up the hole from the twisted stomach surgery.

Beef cows didn't twist often, but it wasn't uncommon for dairy cows, especially those that didn't get enough roughage in their diet.

Before she did surgery, since it was so hard for cows to come up to a good milk production afterward, she always tried to roll them first.

She'd already been out to Raymond Sparrow's farm and rolled the cow.

The bad part about rolling was that it didn't always work. And a vet really couldn't know for sure if it had, or the stomach could twist again, since there was no way to tack the stomach down, since there was no incision.

Regardless of what happened, since this was the second twist visit for this cow, Mabel was doing the actual surgery.

Lark had been on a call already, and she'd called Mabel just to see if she would be available to go out.

Mabel had wanted to stay and talk to James. She...couldn't believe she was engaged. But she didn't want Lark to be out until all hours of the night. She already did more than what she should.

Then, Lark had gotten done with her call and stopped in to see if Mabel needed a hand.

Raymond was one of two dairy farmers in the area. The other dairy farmer never called them. Mabel wasn't sure what vet he used, but it wasn't Lark.

Once she had asked Lark about it, since she found it odd, since for him to use a different vet would mean the vet would need to come from much further away, since she and Lark were the only vets in the area.

Lark, who typically answered questions with a smile and laugh and as much information as Mabel wanted to hear, had shrugged off the question and changed the subject. It was so unlike Lark that Mabel hadn't gotten up the nerve to ask again.

Whatever the issue was between Lark and that farmer, it was more than what Mabel wanted to know, if it made Lark so unhappy.

Mr. Sparrow came by, giving the cow a little more grain.

Surgery for twisted stomachs didn't require complete sedation of the cow, just a general numbing of the area where she would make the incisions. The cow was standing up, held by a stanchion and waiting. She appreciated Mr. Sparrow keeping her calm and fed. Although, she wanted to remind him that his cows needed roughage and they wouldn't twist as easily.

Lark and she had both told Mr. Sparrow that more than once, but he was stuck on his percentages of protein, and cost per pound, and had figured out that grain was the most cost-effective way to get the cow into production and producing at the optimum level.

Most likely he was right, but this surgery was going to set his cow back for the entire lactation period.

"Thanks for coming out on such short notice. This is my top producer, and I wanted to get her straightened up."

"No problem. It's always nice to come out here," Mabel said, pulling the suture through the hide.

Lark gave her a hand holding the hide together but still smiled at Mr. Sparrow.

"Your cows are tame, and it's always a pleasure to work with them," Lark said.

Mr. Sparrow called a thank you over his shoulder as he walked out of the stable.

It was getting to be rather late in the afternoon and was probably time for him to start the evening milking.

That did not make Mabel hurry. She understood from experience that anything that made her hurry would probably end up also making her make a mistake. She didn't do her best work while being rushed. She tried to avoid rushing as much as possible.

"I heard from the grandmother of the three girls while I was on call. I didn't want to tell you in front of Mr. Sparrow, but she said that she was selling her house and just had a buyer put an offer on it yesterday. She's looking forward to getting a place for the girls immediately, since she's moving to a retirement community, and they are not allowed there."

"You're not gonna believe this, but I'm engaged."

"I don't believe it," Lark said with a laugh.

"It's true. It's also true that I shot a man today."

"What?" Lark said, the shock in her voice declaring plainly that she couldn't believe it. "Tell me you're joking."

"No. It's the truth. And I'm engaged to the man I shot."

"You know, pointing a gun at someone and telling them that they have to marry you is not exactly what I had in my mind when I talked about a marriage of convenience."

"That's not exactly how it happened, and to be perfectly honest, I never even considered that. Although, I can't say I wouldn't have gotten desperate enough to actually try it, but it's not necessary now, since like I said, I'm engaged."

She couldn't believe it. She was engaged.

And to James. She barely knew the man before that day.

At the very least, she would have thought she would have gotten engaged to one of the farmers she saw regularly.

Mr. Sparrow, for instance. He was a good bit older than she was, but his wife divorced him years ago and had gone back east.

She hadn't even considered Mr. Sparrow when she'd been thinking about potential husbands, but he would have made a good one.

He probably would have appreciated having a vet as a wife too, because it would save him a lot of money on the vet bills.

"All right. You're going to have to tell me the story."

So, Mabel launched into exactly what happened, down to the fact that she had to bandage James's foot, make him promise to stay off it, and then left him.

"I would never have called you if I would have known all of that was going on."

"I'm glad you did. I would have hated for you to have been out late tonight, when I could easily run out here and do this."

"But you're getting married!" Lark exclaimed. "Congratulations! When did you say the day was?"

"I didn't. We haven't even gotten to talk about that."

"Wow. That's crazy. I guess, when I'd had the idea in my head of a marriage of convenience, I'd kinda thought that was going to be a hold your nose and do it kind of thing, but James is quite a catch."

"I know. Isn't he?" Mabel said, and maybe her words sounded just a little dreamy. She'd been running that over in her head for a while. James. He was handsome and successful and funny and kind and considerate. And he was willing to marry her.

Not that she was the most terrible person in the world, but she just didn't expect it. Didn't think that someone who was so personable and socially adept would be interested in someone like her who was happier sitting in a corner. And he knew that since he'd been to enough business meetings with her dad to know that was her preference.

She wasn't a teenager anymore, but she still had a tendency to navigate to corners and to make herself invisible.

"It sounds to me like maybe you want to plan for a very short engagement. If the girls' grandmother has an offer on her house, you probably have a month, two tops."

"I don't know what he's thinking. I guess I'm okay getting married just as soon as we need to. I mean, it's not really going to make a difference, is it?"

"No. I guess it probably won't. It's going to be an interesting situation though. A new husband, three new children, and a new house you're living in. Are you still going to live with Carol?"

"I don't know!" Mabel said, pulling the last suture tight, looking at her handiwork, and deciding it looked pretty good.

She wouldn't win any awards for her artistry, but she was pretty sure this cow was going to make it.

"I guess we have a lot of things to talk about. And I'll have a captive audience, since I shot him and he can't go anywhere. He's probably afraid if he does, I'll shoot him again." She couldn't even believe she was laughing about accidentally shooting someone.

Again she thought that's probably why she should just stay away from firearms, but she knew that James was correct. She shouldn't avoid things she was afraid of, or not good at, but rather get closer to them, understand them, master them, so that they didn't master her.

That just seemed to be a reasonable thing.

As Lark finished up, and she filled out a bill for Mr. Sparrow and handed it to him, with his promise of payment in the mail next week, they left together, laughing and talking.

Normally, up until a month ago, they would have gone home together, taking care of the girls that were staying at Lark's. But now, with Mabel having moved, they parted at their respective vehicles, with Lark leaving to go home and Mabel leaving to...meet her fiancé.

She was engaged. Unbelievable.

Chapter 11

W hen James saw Mabel pulling into the drive, he was sorely tempted to go meet her. After all, wasn't that what a man was supposed to do with his fiancée?

But he'd made a promise, so he made himself sit still.

He didn't know how much time it normally took Mabel to make it through the house, but it was less than a minute later when she called out the door, "Hey! I'm home. I hope you don't mind if I run up and take a shower quick? I need it."

"Yeah. You've needed that since this morning."

"Hey, I managed to get myself engaged today despite that." She sounded affronted.

"Only because you shot the man and left him no choice."

"Oh my goodness. Is that the way you're telling the story now? With little regard for actual facts?"

He heard her laughing as her steps flew up the stairs.

He chuckled to himself. Of the many things he admired about Mabel, he hadn't really thought much about her sense of humor. He was gratified to find she enjoyed laughing and was able to joke with him.

It was less than fifteen minutes later when she came back downstairs and pushed open the screen door.

"I know I should be helping Carol, but she told me to go shower and spend some time with you. That you've been sitting here all day and you're probably bored out of your mind."

"Well, I think I'm still in my mind, but she's right about me being bored. But I made a promise, and I haven't moved from this porch. Not even once."

"Not even to go to the bathroom?" she asked incredulously.

"Actually, now that you mention it..."

"Oh my goodness. You turkey."

"Well, I've had to go for a while, but I kind of figured that it would be nicer to put my arm around my fiancée than my aunt. So I convinced myself I could wait."

"I think there was a compliment in there somewhere."

"Oh, I know there was." She'd already agreed to marry him. She was laughing and joking with him. And she didn't seem inclined to change her mind. Maybe he could let her know just a little about how he felt.

He didn't want to give too much away. They had a lot of things to hash out.

"All right, I can give you a hand. Do you think you can stand up without putting any weight on it?"

"I think so."

He pulled himself up using the swing's chain and didn't have any trouble balancing on one foot.

She came over and put her arm around his waist, on the opposite side as his hurt foot.

It was a little awkward as they figured out a way that worked, with him barely touching his toes down to get through the step and putting a lot of his weight on her.

She was sturdy and felt warm but still soft beside him, and he really didn't want to be using her as a crutch. He wanted to wrap his arms around her and do a little snuggling.

He supposed that would come in time.

She opened the door and held it with her shoulder while they limped through together.

"I hope you don't mind, but I took the liberty of talking to the pastor. I know from past experience that he likes to do four weeks of marriage counseling before he marries anyone. I... I didn't want to wait that long."

"No. Not if the children need a home now."

"Exactly. And Lark just said that their grandmother just got an offer on her house, and she's moving to an assisted care facility. We have a month, maybe two, but I don't think it's going to take that long."

"I'm good with your timeframe," he said, meaning it.

They were almost at the restroom.

"So the pastor's coming out to eat supper, and then he's going to do marriage counseling with us this evening. If that's okay?"

He stumbled a little and put more weight than what he intended on her shoulders. "Tonight?"

"I can cancel if it's a problem."

"No. I just... I guess that makes it real."

"Yes. I'm sorry if that's pushing it too hard, we can totally reschedule. In fact, let me do that. I would have talked to you about it first, but I left without getting your phone number."

"I guess that's what happens when you get shot and engaged on the same day. Your mind just doesn't think about things like actually being in touch with your fiancée."

"Seriously? Are you going to use that as an excuse?"

"You know, if I had been the one to shoot you, I would be feeling remorse right now."

"You are! You're going to be using this for the next twenty years. Everything bad that ever happens will be the result of the fact that I shot you!"

"Well, it is a pretty traumatic experience. And I think twenty years might be a little bit on the low side. I'm aiming for at least fifty. I think we could probably make seventy if you've got good genes. Do you?"

She laughed. "I think I might die of stress. Being engaged to you is harder than I anticipated."

"Hopefully there will be some benefits to make up for that," he said, and he didn't wink at her, but he wanted to.

She raised her brows. "Benefits? I'm interested."

"Well, I've never been told that I'm a good kisser, but I'm willing to practice until my fiancée thinks I'm talented in that area."

"Willing to practice? Interesting. I wonder who you'd be practicing on?" she said as he stumbled into the bathroom, and before he could answer, she closed the door on him.

That was probably just as well. He basically just admitted to her that he was looking forward to kissing her. Which was the honest-to-goodness truth, but maybe he shouldn't have said it so boldly. He was going to try not to be pushy. So much for that idea.

He probably should be more concerned about the pastor coming though. The idea of marriage counseling scared him to death. The pastor was probably going to give him a bunch of assignments that he would have no idea how to do. And he'd be asking questions that he had no idea of how to answer.

He needed to pull himself together. He'd faced plenty of difficult circumstances, with board members staring down a long table at him and all the pressure on him to perform.

Or at business lunches where he had been trying to close the deal, with his dad insisting that he needed to make profit.

Somehow, despite the fact that the pressure should have been harder for the business, he felt more nervous now.

He had his hand on the doorknob when his phone buzzed in his pocket.

Pulling it out, he swiped to answer.

"Hello?"

"James. The transition isn't going as smoothly as what I had hoped. After you left, we met with some resistance from a few people we have in key positions, and I think we're going to need you back here. I'm not sure for how long."

It was his second-in-command and trusted business partner, Richard.

His words made James's stomach hurt.

"I can't come today. I can't actually come for a week. I did something to my foot, and the doctor recommended complete and total rest."

"Bed rest for a foot injury?" Richard sounded incredulous.

He supposed he could find crutches if he needed them. "No. I have to stay off my foot."

"Then just use your crutches."

"Yeah. I'll do that if I have to, but I'd rather not. I want this to heal correctly. And the doc is concerned about infection."

"All right. Just don't say I didn't warn you. I highly recommend you come back as soon as you can. Tonight preferably, tomorrow if you have to delay that long."

"All right. I'll see what I can do, but just do your best to hold things together until I can get there."

He had planned on using the money from his business to support them for the rest of his life. He had also planned on handing it over to other people to manage so that he wouldn't have to spend every waking hour, night, day, and weekend to keep things going. He had done that for years, and after his dad had retired and moved to the Florida Keys with his fourth wife, James had figured he'd done his duty and was free to hand things over. Maybe pursue some of those things that he might have been interested in once upon a time but hadn't been given the freedom to do.

Farming being one of them. He could remember when he was quite small wanting to drive a tractor. But that was probably something every little boy had a hankering to do at some point.

Still, the grown-up version of himself did not have an aversion to doing that. Not if he had a wife like Mabel beside him.

Twisting the handle, he opened the door, shocked to see Mabel standing on the other side.

"Sorry. I had a call."

"I could hear, a little bit anyway. Is everything okay?"

"It was my business partner, Richard. He wants me to go back to Chicago. I...don't want to."

"It is necessary, I understand. We can talk about that, but we probably ought to get a few things together before the pastor gets here. I feel bad that I suggested that he come, but I thought we were in agreement on moving forward."

"We are," he said immediately, not wanting her to get the idea that he wanted to delay anything. He did not.

"All right. I feel like I'm pushing you though."

"You're not. Should we go into the kitchen and help Aunt Carol, or should we go out to the porch swing?"

"I talked to her for just a few minutes while you were in the restroom, and she said she has everything in hand. I think she wants us to get this hashed out. She wants to be able to tell her friends, but right now all she can say is that we're engaged, but she has no idea about any details. She wants the details." Mabel laughed as she helped him hobble to the front door.

"All right. Let's get some details hashed out for Aunt Carol."

They laughed together as he made his way to the porch swing and sat back down.

"I love porch swings, but I spent a little bit too much time on one today."

"At least you have a beautiful view. So much sky, so much waving grass. And the temperature today was absolutely perfect for sitting outside."

"You're right on all three counts." He slid a little bit, giving her room to sit down, which she did. Lifting his bandaged foot, he propped it on his opposite knee and stretched his arm out across the back of the porch swing. He didn't touch her, but he was tempted to.

"All right. How soon are we going to get married?" he said, figuring he might as well lead off the conversation. He wasn't going to beat around the bush, and she was right about needing to get some details figured out. It didn't seem very romantic to him, but Mabel didn't seem like the kind of woman who needed a lot of romance. Maybe he was wrong about that, but he thought that possibly his loyalty to her and his willingness to do things for her would count for more in her book than a bunch of flowers and pretty words. In fact, he was quite sure that the pretty words weren't going to mean anything to her if he didn't back them up with actions.

"A week? I actually was thinking tomorrow, but I figured there were probably people that you'd like to have here?"

"My dad might come up from the Keys. With my third step-mother."

"Third?" she asked, wrinkling her nose.

"Yeah. After my mom died, he couldn't seem to find anyone that would...stay with him? Put up with him? I'm not sure which of the two is correct, but he's on his third wife, actually fourth if you count my mom. It's my third stepmother."

"I'm so sorry. That must be hard."

"Not really. This one's been the easiest, because he married her right before he retired and moved to the Keys. I don't have to see them very often. The second one was the worst, and I actually kind of liked the first one. I was younger then, though. Maybe I wasn't as cynical and couldn't see through the façade that showed that she was all about his money and definitely not about his happiness."

"Wow. That's hard. And I guess I can see how that would make you cynical."

"Yeah. I try not to be, but I guess that's just something that happens whenever you have money. And people know it. They...want a piece of it, you know?"

"Or a piece of you."

"You actually did get a piece of me earlier today."

"Seriously? Is every conversation going to go back to that?"

"I told you. It's a pretty momentous occasion in a person's life when they get shot."

"You know what, I'm going to march right in that house, grab that case from Carol, and insist you shoot me. And then, we'll both have something to talk about."

"Nah. I like being the only one in the relationship who's gotten shot. I think I'll keep it that way."

"You are no help."

He grinned, his boyish, engaging grin, and he was right, she couldn't resist it, and she grinned right back at him.

His heart warmed, and he had the feeling that with all the things that happened today—and they still had a long evening ahead of them if they were going to entertain the preacher and get marriage counseling—it had been a good day. A very good day.

Chapter 12

Mabel sat on the porch swing, tucking her feet up underneath her and resting her hands in her lap.

It was nice to get out of her work clothes, to get the smell of cow manure off her, and sit in peace on the swing.

A beautiful view, a beautiful evening, and...someone she was really starting to like beside her.

That scared her just a little bit. The idea of getting married was scary enough, but getting married to someone she cared about was even more scary for some odd reason. Probably because she was afraid that he would not care for her the way she cared for him, and she would end up getting hurt. It was that old issue she dealt with in childhood. The one she had worked so hard to overcome.

It felt like she was taking a very big risk to start to like James as more than a casual acquaintance.

It was bound to happen. He was insisting on a real marriage, and she had to agree with him.

Swallowing her fear, she looked over at him. "So we're both willing to do it sooner, but a week is good?"

"Sure. Let's plan on that. You heard the conversation I had on the phone, and I might have to go to Chicago. I told him I had to stay off my foot," he said, giving her a look that said that he would do his very best to obey her orders.

"I'm sure I can dig you up a pair of crutches, if you need to go. In fact, you shouldn't have to be stuck on the front porch swing all day long every day for the next week. You need a pair anyway."

"I can probably make myself something."

"I'm pretty sure Hines Cannon broke his leg not long ago. I think he might have crutches, and I'm sure I can borrow them, if he doesn't outright give them to us, which he probably will."

"All right. Maybe after the pastor leaves, if there's still time, we can take a ride out."

"Sure. Let me text Eliza and see." Her fingers flew over her phone as she sent a quick text. She wasn't best friends with Eliza, but they knew each other fairly well and liked each other too.

"So are we going to tell the preacher that this is a marriage of convenience? He's sure to ask us about love and all that other stuff that he probably expects from people he's giving marriage counseling to."

Mabel let out a long breath. She wanted to sigh and put her head in her hands.

"I don't want to lie or mislead the preacher," she finally said. "But you're right, it's going to be an awkward conversation."

"I'm sure Aunt Carol will help us if we need her to."

"Yes. I'm sure she will. And I guess if he has issues with it, we'll deal with that when we get to them."

She knew that they were doing something rash that a lot of people would frown on. It didn't feel rash to her though. It felt like a wise move. Like they were doing something to create a home for three girls who needed it, and that they had talked about it like adults and made a firm decision.

She supposed that the world's idea of spending years getting to know someone was necessary if people did not plan on sticking to their vows no matter what. She felt from a carnal perspective that it was probably foolish, because most couples who spent years together ended up committing fornication before their marriage.

She supposed it was just another way of the world trying to impose their wisdom above and beyond what God commanded.

Trying to insist that man's wisdom was somehow better than God's commands.

Not that she ever thought long and hard along those lines, but it just made sense to her, that two people of character could make a smart decision and then get married without a whole lot of fanfare.

"I kept thinking all day that there were so many things for us to talk about, and now that we're sitting here, I can't think of a single one," Mabel said, twisting her hands together.

Maybe her nervousness was obvious, because James reached over and placed his hand over top of hers. "We've got plenty of time. We'll be fine."

Somehow, the feeling of his warm hand over top of hers made the tension that had been building in her body drain out. She looked up at him, the relief on her face plain for him to see, she was sure.

"You're right. We don't have to stress about this."

"No. What is it about women and weddings that seems to bring out the stress hormone in everyone?"

"I'm sure you've seen some fancy ones," she murmured. Just then, it hit her how much different he was than she. He had been brought up with money and prestige, and while she had too, ever since her parents had died, she had lived a quiet life in not exactly poverty, but definitely a lot more frugally than she had when her parents had been taking her all over the country, giving the illusion that they had money, when it was all a house of cards.

She would much rather live honestly than try to show off, acting like she had more than what she had just to give people... What was it? To somehow make herself look better than what she was. She didn't really understand the point of that.

It had been important to her parents, at any rate.

Finding out the truth had been difficult for both her and her sister. Gladys had honestly probably suffered more than she had.

But it had been a hard truth for both of them.

"I'm sure you have, too. Back in the day," James said casually.

"Don't you want to have a big, fancy wedding?"

"No. I don't. I was thinking if my dad came, that might be two more people than what I actually want to have there. But you could hardly not invite your parent to your wedding, could you?"

"I always thought you had a good relationship with your dad."

"I feel like I do. Although, he did demand a lot out of me. Looking back, I'm glad he did, it made me a better person, but at the time, I didn't appreciate it."

"I guess that's kind of the way it is with the people in our childhood, right? Because growing always hurts."

"Always?"

"I think so. Don't you?"

He seemed to think about that for a while, and she tried to come up with a scenario that would make a person grow but wouldn't also inflict pain. It was hard for her to come up with anything. Anytime a person got better, it was usually because they went through something that was hard.

"Unless a person really likes things like practicing, or reps in the gym, or burning food, or learning that friends can be brutally honest or heartbreakingly dishonest..."

"I guess you're right. Maybe not physical pain, but mental pain, and then you have to work your way through it. I hadn't quite thought about it in those terms before, but you're right. Growth involves pain, and that's why we resist it so much in our childhood and teen years. And that's why they seem so hard. We're doing a lot of growing, a lot of learning, which involves a lot of hurting."

"And it makes us tired too. I remember being so tired when I was a teenager," she said, leaning her head back against the edge of the swing.

She forgot he put his arm there, and instead of meeting the back of the swing, her head landed on his arm.

She popped back up right away.

"I'm sorry," she said. "I didn't mean to do that."

"It's fine. I didn't mind at all."

He had that tone again. The one he'd used before, the one that made a shot of something warm and sweet curl along her backbone and something smooth slide through her chest.

She looked at him a little longer than she meant to, and then, deliberately, she laid her head back down.

"You're not a teenager anymore but you're still allowed to be tired." His murmured words held a hint of humor but also more than a little hint of that heart-curling whatever it was. The tone that made her feel like maybe he cared for her more than someone who had just met her today would be expected to.

It was an odd feeling and one she wanted to talk to him about. But she didn't know how to start the conversation. What was she going to say—*how do you feel about me?*

"I think that might be the pastor coming," James said after a few beats of silence.

She turned her head, still leaning against his forearm, to see a car coming up the drive.

"Yeah. I think that's him. We're good?" she asked, feeling the tightening of her stomach as nervousness took over.

"I know it will work out. Whatever we do, we'll handle it together. And we're going to tell the truth, so there's no need to coordinate lies. And if he doesn't like it, we'll just deal with it. But it's not going to upset us."

"That sounds perfect to me."

"Is that the preacher coming?" Carol said as she appeared outlined against the screen, a dishrag in her hand.

"It is, are you ready?"

"I was thinking maybe you would do your marriage counseling first. The chicken I put in the oven still has another thirty minutes."

"All right. I'll go meet him and tell him to come on around here."

"I hate that I can't go with you."

"I love that you're listening," she said with a smug look as she opened the screen door and followed Carol through the house.

She met the preacher as he was getting out of his car and shook his hand, welcoming him to the house.

"James is on the front porch. I don't know whether I mentioned it or not, but he hurt his foot today, and I advised him to stay off it as much as possible."

"All right. You had mentioned it, but that's not a problem. I think I smell fried chicken," he said as they walked around the house.

"Baked chicken, from what it sounded like, but it sure smells good, doesn't it?"

"It sure does. If you tell me how long it's going to be until it's ready, I can probably pare my marriage counseling down so it fits in just nicely. My stomach is growling. And trying to gnaw a hole through my backbone."

Mabel laughed, liking that the pastor was a simple man who didn't get worked up about things. She figured she was probably borrowing trouble to think he was going to have a problem with their speedy marriage.

As they stepped up the front porch steps, she said, "This is James. James, this is our local pastor, he has the white church in Sweet Water."

"Good to meet you, sir. I'd stand up, but my nurse here told me that I need to stay off my foot."

"I see," the pastor said, grasping James's hand and looking at the bandages around his foot.

"What happened?" he said as Mabel arranged a chair for him to sit on and then settled herself down beside James.

"She shot me," James said casually.

"Mabel shot you?" The pastor's eyes bugged out. Then he huffed out a breath. "Was that before or after you asked her to marry you?"

"It was before. I think she used a lot of intimidation."

"Would you please be serious? He s never going to marry us if he thinks you were coerced into it. And we both know that's not the case."

"She's right. She didn't mean to shoot me. It was an accident."

"You're saying she shot you with a gun?" the pastor said, feeling the need to clarify apparently.

"It was a gun that belonged to Annie Oakley, and she seemed quite enamored with it, but she obviously had no idea of how to handle it."

"Obviously."

"Yes."

The pastor raised his brows. "I don't usually recommend prenups, but I might suggest that, or make sure that someone else is the beneficiary of your life insurance."

"Oh my goodness," Mabel said, only a little outraged but laughing too. "I promise, I had no intention of actually hitting anyone or anything, and I'm definitely not the beneficiary of his life insurance. We just decided to get married today."

"Today? So that's a little fast," the pastor said slowly.

"Yes. Considering that we just met for the first time today, although we knew each other from her dad and I working together. Today was the first day we had any conversations of any length."

"And now you're getting married?" the pastor clarified. "After she shot you."

"That really had nothing to do with it," James said easily, grinning at Mabel and easing her fears. "We decided a marriage of convenience would be a good idea. That was after she decided that I was a man of character who would keep my word. I already knew that she was a woman of integrity, whom I could trust and who would be loyal."

"I see, and what caused you to decide this marriage of convenience was a good idea?" the pastor asked.

"There are three girls who need a home," Mabel began, giving him the story and the reasoning behind their decision.

The pastor steepled his hands together and listened intently as she spoke. "There seems to be a rash of these things going on around in Sweet Water the past few years, and I have to say, I was very skeptical with the first few, but then, as I saw how they worked out, I'm not quite as skeptical as I used to be. In fact, I would almost recommend this type of marriage to people. When you enter into a relationship rationally, with the decision that no matter what happens, you're going to stick it out, your marriage has a much better chance of lasting."

That shocked Mabel to her toes. It was not what she was expecting to hear, and she couldn't have been more happy.

"Now, I can smell that chicken from here, so if you don't mind, I'd like to get down to business."

Chapter 13

T he pastor lifted his brows in question, but he got no argument from Mabel or James.

"I do usually like to spend a little bit more time on marriage counseling, but like I said, I've had more than a few of these over the years, and I'll do my best to condense what I need to say into one session. Although, if you're willing to come see me after you get married, you're certainly welcome to. Marriage is one of my favorite topics, and it's an institution ordained by God, between a man and woman, in order for them to create a home and raise children. I definitely think we need to keep the nature of marriage sacred and treat it as the covenant that it is. We have a tendency to take it too lightly in our world today."

The pastor steepled his fingers, then leaned forward a little bit before checking his notes. "I like to talk about love. I like to talk about commitment. I even like to talk about kindness, because marriage entails all of those things. But today, for some reason, I feel compelled to talk about humility."

He gave a little smile. "I don't think either one of you have a problem in this area, but I do think that sometimes we have a tendency to think in our modern world that humility is an antiquated character trait."

The pastor raised his brows as though giving a warning. "I submit to you that nothing could be further from the truth. God values humility. In fact, if you read the Bible, you'll notice that He often chooses humble people in order to further His work. Why do you think Jesus was born in a stable? It was a humble beginning. Because God was giving us an example. Jesus was a carpenter's son, he had no education, no money, no connections, no claim to fame, none of the things that our society today values, and nothing society back then thought was important. Money, friends, prestige, family connections. He wasn't even from a town that had a reputation for anything other than paganism and wretchedness. The question is asked, can anything good come out of Nazareth? That was the town Jesus was from. Even his town was humble."

The pastor pressed his lips together and smiled a little, as though knowing that what he was saying would be hard. "Humility is hard. It goes against our grain. It's not something that we want to do in our flesh, it has to be because of our love for Jesus. Why else would someone deliberately humble themselves?" The pastor took a breath. "But yet, humility can cause two people who otherwise might not get along to be best friends."

He tilted his head a little as though thinking about his words. "First of all, humility is not necessarily shrugging off praise. Although, it can be. Sometimes people will say that it's not turning away from accolades, and yet, a humble person doesn't seek praise and doesn't necessarily bask in it. We all appreciate a kind word and perhaps strive for those awards, but to the humble person, that's not the main reason they do what they do. Humility is more allowing yourself to come in last. Whether it's a race, a competition, or whatever. In other words, in a marriage, you are totally willing to stand behind the other person, and rather than using them to make you look good and expecting them to serve you and lift you up, you do that for them. Pride is what makes us want to use others to lift ourselves up. Humility is what allows us to do that for our spouse and for the people around us. We don't keep score, we don't keep track, and we don't have our ego and our self-worth dependent on 'beating' other people. That's especially bad in a marriage, when it becomes a competition to see who can be the best rather than a competition to see who can be the best servant."

That resonated with Mabel. Maybe that was why she and Lark got along so well. Because Lark wasn't just happy and affable almost all the time, but she was also one of the most humble people Mabel knew. She was the senior vet and had been the whole time that Mabel had known her, but even before Mabel had gotten her doctorate degree and passed her licensing test, Lark had treated her as an equal. It had never been about Lark making a name for herself.

As Mabel sat there, she realized that Lark had set the tone for their relationship. And she had followed along, not making it a competition to see who could be better but always working for the good of everyone else.

She glanced at James. She didn't even know what he did in his business. Could she work to lift him up? Could she put herself aside?

She knew she could do that for the girls. She'd done it while they were there before. But humility for children was one thing. Humility for your spouse was something completely different. Especially if he was not humble in return.

As though the pastor could read her thoughts, he said, "We have a tendency to think to ourselves 'if' this or 'if' that. In other words, I'll be humble. I'll be a servant. I'll serve, I'll put myself under, but then expect other people to do the same for us. When it doesn't happen, we take ourselves out of that humble position, and either walk away, or demand that the other person reciprocate the behavior that we performed."

The pastor leaned back in his chair, and it rocked slowly. "Jesus did not do that. He never demanded that his disciples be as humble as he was. He was always willing to be the most humble. And he never rubbed it in. If you look at his life, he never once, not one time, held up the trump card and said, 'I'm the son of God, so you need to fill in the blank here,' did he?" The pastor looked at both of them, and they slowly shook their heads.

Mabel didn't know what James was thinking, but she definitely knew the pastor had hit on something that she absolutely could work on. Because, while she didn't have a problem being humble, she did expect people to be humble in return.

Maybe Lark had spoiled her a little bit.

"That's our goal. To be humble, without expecting it in return. Of course, that's the goal in the Christian life in general, isn't it? To love without being loved in return, to be kind without having someone be kind to us in return, to act the way God wants us to act, no matter how the people around us are acting. In my opinion, humility is especially hard for me to achieve when others around me are acting wrong."

The pastor pressed his lips together, and then he continued, "Humility apologizes first. Humility admits that you're wrong, even when you feel the other person is just as wrong as you are, humility doesn't need credit for your work, humility allows you to step back and let someone else who maybe doesn't deserve it step forward. Humility allows you to work for someone else's glory and not your own. Humility is happy when others succeed and does not resent their success."

The pastor looked down at his Bible before he looked back up. "I can tell you guys this, but know that I am also preaching to myself. This is something I struggle with. I don't want to be the only one admitting that I'm wrong. And if I do, I want credit for it. I want to know people notice. I want to know that my wife notices. I want her to appreciate me and compliment me, I want her to make me look good when we go places."

His smile was sheepish but sincere, and Mabel admired him for admitting to his weakness.

"I suppose you can boil humility down to the fact that you put others first. That's being humble. But you can take it so much further. Because you can still put others first while grabbing attention for yourself. Or you can serve others and then make sure that everyone around you knows it."

He smiled and chuckled just a little. "It always amazes me how God perfectly set up a woman to become exactly what He wants. After all, children do not give you credit for what you do. They don't thank you for getting up in the middle of the night and changing their diaper and feeding them. They don't appreciate the fact that you've cleaned up the mess that they made every day for the last five years. They don't give you credit for anything that they accomplish; they like to think they did it on their own. They don't remember that Mom taught them to talk, to walk, and made sure they got up and went to school every day." He lifted his brows. "And you two are bringing children into your home. That's going to be quite an adjustment and is going to be an exercise in humility from both of you, because neither one of you is going to be able to do what you're used to being able to do. And neither one of you is going to get the credit that you deserve."

Mabel realized that from her small experience over the winter with the children. They didn't typically thank her, although she had the feeling that they were slightly more appreciative than normal kids might be, since they knew what it was like to be completely neglected. As she understood it, before their mother had gone to jail, they had been alone in the house more often than not.

Still, she appreciated what the pastor was saying and figured that if she were able to be humble, no matter what happened, her marriage would work.

Even if a spouse cheated, it took humility to be able to forgive and to put that behind them.

She wasn't sure whether she had quite that much humility, but anything up to that point, to forgive, to look past the hurt and disappointments, that all required humility.

"All right, do either of you have any questions?" the pastor said, sniffing the air appreciatively.

Beside her, she felt the swing shake a little as James laughed. She was sure he was doing the same thing, sniffing the air and thinking about chicken.

"I appreciate the reminder. I definitely could use it," Mabel said, which made the pastor smile.

"I didn't even go into that. How being able to take correction with a smile, with gratefulness, is a sign of humility. And being able to surrender our will to someone else's, whether it's the Lord, or our spouse, by giving up our way and picking up someone else's way without complaining, is a great sign of humility."

"It's something I struggle with as well," James agreed. "A good reminder, and one that I kept thinking would really be beneficial to our marriage. After all, if we are both humble, there's hardly any way we wouldn't get along."

Mabel nodded, and the pastor opened his mouth to say something, but Carol appeared at the door.

"I hope you guys are hungry. Supper's ready."

"I'm starving," the pastor said, not exactly jumping out of his chair but moving a little quicker than he had when he sat down.

Mabel had to admit she was moving faster too, and James's arm around her, although it felt just as heavy and just as good, didn't seem to slow them down quite as much as it had before.

Of course, maybe they were getting used to hobbling around together, but food had a way of inspiring a person to find a way to move a little faster.

The pastor went in first, and James tightened his grip on her shoulders, squeezing her to him and leaning his head down.

"He didn't scare you out of making a commitment to me, did he?" he asked, his words close to her ear and sending a shiver down through her body.

"No. On the contrary, it made me more eager to get started. I like a good challenge, and being humble is definitely a challenge."

"I'll agree with that. Although, you don't really strike me as someone who has a lot of trouble staying humble."

"I like to do things my way. I like to set my own course, and I'm rather independent. I suppose, that's not exactly pride, but it definitely makes being humble, submitting myself to someone else's thoughts and ideas, a lot harder."

"Well, I'm not going to demand that you do what I want you to do. In fact, I was really hoping that I could let go of the reins of my business and stay out here full-time. I... I had never considered being a dad before, but I guess that idea has been kind of nipping at the edges of my thoughts all day."

"Really?" She couldn't believe it. She'd been wondering how they were going to juggle the kids, with her job and his job, and whether they'd get a nanny or hire someone full-time or how they would do that.

"I wanted to talk with you first. But honestly, I have no idea how to be a dad. I mean, I've had my dad's example, but I wouldn't say it's a good one. Maybe it's more of a blueprint of things that I don't want to do, but I'm willing to learn."

"I don't have any better idea of how to be a mom. I've seen Lark, but I think my parents' example was probably just as bad as yours. They were much more concerned about looks and prestige than they were about actual character. They talked the talk, but they never walked the walk and in fact built a house of cards that collapsed shortly after their death."

She didn't blame them for it and didn't hold it against them, but she wanted better than that for her own children.

Speaking of children. "I'd like to adopt the girls if we can."

"Yeah. I wasn't thinking that, but I was definitely thinking that they were going to be our children. If not legally, at least that's the way we would treat them."

"If I recall correctly, the mother has already lost her parental rights, and the grandmother has guardianship. If she approves of us, it might be a simple, straightforward thing." She hardly dared to hope that would actually happen. Adoptions typically were not simple nor straightforward, and one involving three girls would probably be a lot more complicated than one involving just one child.

"All right. I actually have several lawyers on my team. They're not exactly well-versed in adoption law, but they might be able to connect us with some people who can make the process as painless as possible."

"That would be amazing," she said, smiling with relief. She had to admit having someone beside her was so much better than trying to do everything by herself. Which, up to that point in her life, had pretty much been the way it was.

She wasn't always a great team player. She liked to do things her way. She hadn't been kidding when she said that to him earlier. But in return for being a team player, she had someone on her team. It seemed obvious, but she liked the payoff. At least now.

"Come on. I know you're hungry, and that chicken is calling you." She grinned.

"It sure is. I've forgotten what a great cook Aunt Carol is. I'm not sure why I ever moved away."

"Oh. Well, about that. That whole cooking thing. I... I'm not a good cook." That was the understatement of the year. She could boil water. And she might be able to throw chicken on a tray and put it in the oven, but to actually make it taste good might be a whole different concept.

"Awesome. We found a flaw. And here I was starting to think you're perfect."

She laughed, but she didn't think from looking at his face that he was kidding. It made her feel good down to her toes, mostly because she didn't think he would just say the words without meaning them. He hadn't given her a bunch of empty flattery up until that point, and she was pretty sure that this was not him starting. Rather, it was him telling her something sincere, and she appreciated that as they hobbled into the house together.

Chapter 14

Was rain on one's wedding day a bad omen?

James couldn't remember if that was a thing or not as he paced in the small room off to the side of the pulpit of the church in town.

He and Mabel had both agreed that they would prefer their wedding be in a church.

They also both had wanted the girls to come, but their grandmother had wanted to keep them for one last day. They would be arriving on the farm in the morning.

Mabel had been very disappointed when she found out the girls wouldn't be able to make it. But he appreciated the fact that she hadn't made a big deal about it. She accepted the fact that they wouldn't be there, and that was that. She didn't suggest that they postpone the wedding.

Actually, that suggestion had come from him.

She had denied it immediately. After all, his dad had flown in just for the day, leaving his new wife in the Keys, and Lark had taken off work, and the ladies of the Sweet Water church had decorated the sanctuary.

In other words, a lot of work had been done, and she didn't want to inconvenience everyone, just to make herself happy.

He thought of the pastor's words on humility, and he felt that Mabel was living them today. It wasn't about her, it was about serving everyone else, even though she was the bride.

He hadn't heard her demand anything, and he admired her for that, because, if anyone had a right to demand anything, surely their wedding day gave them that prerogative.

He came to the wall, spun on his heel, which Mabel had just given him permission to walk on, and paced to the other side of the small room.

The pastor calmly sat in a chair in the corner with his eyes on the open scripture in front of him.

James figured he would probably be better off if he opened his own Bible, instead of allowing the thoughts that were racing through his head to have free rein.

He wasn't exactly nervous... That was a lie. He was more nervous than he'd ever been in his life before. But it wasn't necessarily him wondering whether the wedding was a good idea or not, although he thought he would probably be crazy if he wasn't a little bit nervous, considering he was about to make vows that were to last a lifetime.

"Can I help you with anything, son?" the pastor said, lifting his head up and removing his glasses as James crossed the small room once more.

"No. I'm good."

"You seem a little worried." The pastor was pretty good at under-statement. "Marriage is a big step."

"I'm not worried about the marriage necessarily, but it's been a long time since I've made vows that I have to keep for a lifetime."

"You're right to be nervous. Actually, if you weren't, I would be more concerned. After all, the more you mean it, the more significance it has."

"I mean it with everything I have, so I guess that makes this the most significant event of my life."

"Even though it's a marriage of convenience?" the pastor asked, and James figured he was playing devil's advocate. "Are you changing your mind?" the pastor said, and that pretty much confirmed James's thoughts.

"No. I'm not considering for one instant the idea of changing my mind. I just... I just know it's a lot of responsibility. I want to be the very best husband that I can be. I want to be a great dad, I want to be all the things that Mabel deserves. I'm not sure I am, and I'm not sure I ever will be."

"And if she is thinking the same thing, then your marriage has an excellent chance of success. After all, someone who goes into a marriage thinking that the other person is lucky to get them is not going into it with a humble attitude."

"That's true. I'm pretty sure that Mabel is one of the most humble people I know. So I'm not worried about that at all, either."

"Then, if you're sure that this is the Lord's will for your life, I think you have a solid woman in Mabel, and I'm impressed with the way you are too. I think your marriage has every chance of succeeding. And I think you're going to make an amazing husband and a really great father. I say that with confidence, because one of the most important qualities in being a good husband or a good father is the willingness to be teachable, to realize there is much room for improvement, and then work on improving."

The pastor stood, wiping his glasses on his tie and setting his Bible on a shelf.

His words had eased James's mind; they were words he needed, even though he didn't realize it.

"All right, if you're ready, it's time."

He hadn't even realized that the strains of music were the ones to which they were supposed to walk out.

There had been a small rehearsal the night before, basically to show everyone where they stood and to let them know what would be playing when.

Amber, Darby and Jonah's daughter, played the piano, and for some reason, James wondered if any of his girls would want to take lessons.

Children weren't something he had considered in his life before, but he liked the idea that he was starting to think fatherly thoughts, even though the kids hadn't even arrived yet. Hopefully that boded well.

The pastor stood at the end of the aisle, and James took his place beside him. They had decided not to have attendants, just to make things as simple as possible. They didn't want to put any added stress and strain on their friends. They wanted it to be a fun day, a day of celebration, not a day of stress and care.

The strains of music changed again, and the congregation stood. James lifted his eyes and saw his bride walking down the aisle.

She wore a simple peasant shirt and a skirt that swished around her ankles. The shirt was white, but the skirt was green with purple flowers on it. They matched the purple wildflowers she held in her hand and the ones that had been placed throughout her hair which was down.

He racked his brain, trying to think if he'd ever seen her hair down. Normally she wore it in a ponytail or even in a braid, which suited her no-nonsense personality. She wasn't frivolous or cute or even exceptionally feminine.

He bit back a smile as she strode down the aisle, rather than took the graceful little steps of a typical bride.

She walked alone.

He felt bad about that and wondered if she missed her dad. She hadn't said anything in the days leading up to their wedding, but they hadn't talked as much as he had hoped they would.

He'd had to go to Chicago, and he'd done his best to straighten things out. He wasn't sure if he was successful or not, but he wasn't going to let that bother him. If the business didn't do well, if he lost it, he had what mattered right here in North Dakota.

She was walking toward him, and while he hadn't told her he loved her, hadn't even kissed her yet, he thought that maybe he was falling. After all, he'd admired her for years and wanted this day to happen, having no idea that it actually would and much sooner than he anticipated. She clutched the flowers tightly. He could see the whites of her knuckles, and so, when she looked up, meeting his eyes, he smiled at her. He wanted her to know that he was eager and excited. That, and that she was the reason.

He didn't know if he conveyed all of that to her with his smile, but she returned the gesture, and he noted that her grip on the flowers loosened.

The ceremony went by in a blur; the only thing that really anchored him were the hands that he held throughout it.

He brushed her lips with his when the pastor told him to, and the church erupted in cheers.

The reception was potluck, and he was pretty sure that Mabel had a great time. He knew he did. Mostly because they were side by side through it all.

He supposed the feeling would wear off, but he wouldn't mind if she stayed beside him forever.

He figured that was too much to ask, but hopefully, with care and deliberation on their part, their relationship would deepen and blossom into something that closely resembled love, even if it wasn't quite the way the rest of the world did it.

It was at least four hours later when the older ladies of the church shooed them off, telling them that they would make sure that everything got cleaned up and encouraging them to go home and enjoy themselves.

Aunt Carol was staying the night at Miss April's house, in town, which James had never gotten around to thanking her for but made a note to do so.

Not that he had anything planned with Mabel, other than sitting on the front porch and holding her hand.

But shortly after they got in the car, Mabel's phone rang. He hadn't even pulled out of the church parking lot.

"I don't have to get this," she said, lifting her brows at him and holding up her phone. It showed a number with the local area code, but he didn't recognize it.

"Is that someone calling for an emergency?"

"Most likely."

Lark had been called out of the reception an hour previously, for a calf with an intestinal protraction. She probably was not done dealing with that emergency.

"Most likely, he called Lark first, and she told him she couldn't come right away, and I would guess that she told him not to bother me because it was my wedding day."

"Do you know who it is?"

"I have a good idea. But I'm not entirely sure I recognize the number."

"Why don't you answer it? We'll have a unique wedding night, if nothing else."

"Are you sure?"

"Unless you don't want to."

"I'd rather spend it with you, but.. This is my calling." She bit her lip. "And the farmers of Sweet Water depend on me. I... I would like to be able to take off for my wedding, but at the same time, the idea that something might die because I ignored it..."

"Answer it, before it quits ringing."

She didn't need further encouragement, swiped her phone, and said, "Hello?"

He could hear a voice through the phone but couldn't hear what it was saying.

He stopped trying to listen and realized that he wasn't all that upset. This was what Mabel did for a living, he knew it, and he loved that part of her. Part of the reason that he'd never made a move for her earlier was because he knew that this meant a lot to her. Being a vet, taking care of animals, saving lives, it was what she wanted to do. And... Maybe that was humility. Stepping back and allowing her to do what she needed to do, supporting her if necessary. But just letting her know that he wouldn't hold it against her or be upset.

That reminder eased the tiny little bit of irritation that had pulled up in his chest. And he smiled as she hung up.

"It's George Miller, on the other side of Sweet Water, and he has a horse that's colicking. I have a few things I can do for it, and I think we'll be able to save it, but I'll need to hurry."

Her words were calm, she hadn't raised her voice at all, but he could hear the urgency as she spoke.

"All right. You want to go home and change?"

"Yes. I need to grab my bag. I...didn't bring it to our wedding."

"Good. It's good to know that at least you didn't plan this." He winked at her, and she laughed.

"No. I would definitely not have a horse colicking on purpose."

"You know, I kind of feel like I can admit something to you now," he said, even as he sped up, because he didn't want her to lose a horse on their wedding day. That didn't seem to be the best way to start out a marriage, although he wouldn't consider it a bad omen, since he didn't believe in them. He believed in God, which was a whole lot better than depending on something as whimsical as luck.

"Admit something?" she asked, raising her brows way out.

"Yeah. I don't know whether this is going to scare you or make you happy."

"Okay, you're scaring me now," she said, fingering the band that he'd put on her finger not that long ago.

"When your parents died, I came, intending to go to the funeral. I...wanted to pursue a relationship with you at that time. I had wanted to for a while. But your dad and me being in business together was a little bit of an inhibitor, but also the fact that you were so young. Still, with your parents gone, I wanted to step in.

But... I knew that you wanted to be a vet, and I thought that you trying to juggle your studies and a long-distance boyfriend, if I could even get to that point, might be too much. So I backed off."

She turned while he was talking, and her jaw hung open. It was obvious from the look on her face that she had had no idea. "You're kidding, right?"

"No. I'm not. I'm dead serious."

Chapter 15

"All right, you don't need to walk him around. But you can if it seems to make him feel better. Just keep a close eye on him and text me when he has his first bowel movement. Also, let me know if he stops drinking for any length of time. The molasses we put in his water will hopefully make it sweet enough to entice him to consume more than he normally would, but keep that bucket of clean water beside it as well, just in case the molasses water doesn't appeal to him."

Mabel went down over the list of things she needed George to continue to do after she left.

James had been an amazing help. He hadn't barged in or tried to take over, and he hadn't lost interest and wandered away. He had been at her elbow, close enough for her to talk to but not to trip over.

If only she had an assistant like that all the time.

But that wasn't being humble the way the pastor had described it, that was her being proud as she wished for help herself.

Of course, she would do the same for James, if the opportunity ever arose. But they still hadn't completely hashed out what he was going to be doing with his business.

And she had been consumed with wedding and work and kids, and they hadn't really had a chance to talk about it.

How could she become less busy?

The question had been on her mind ever since the phone call that had taken her from the evening that she and James were supposed to spend together and brought her out to the farm to save a horse's life.

She thought the horse was going to be okay. It was calm and was not in distress anymore, although the medication she had given had taken most of the pain away.

But from what she could tell, he would most likely make it.

She knew the odds were just fifty to sixty percent, but she felt pretty confident in this one.

George had gotten a hold of her quickly, and she'd come out as soon as she could. A lot of times, early intervention made all the difference.

As much as she would have loved to have been able to go home and spend a quiet evening with her new husband, the horse probably wouldn't have made it if she had done that.

Struggling but trying not to show it, she finished giving George his instructions and then gave him the bill.

He wrote her out a check, and she gathered her things and got ready to leave.

They had ended up taking her SUV, which was outfitted with all the things she needed in the back. A custom-made tool chest sat in the very back, with drawers where she kept the medications and the instruments that she needed.

It had been a lifesaver more than once.

She thanked George, asked him once more if he had any questions, and then she walked beside her husband to their vehicle.

She got in the passenger seat, and he drove. She was happy to have someone take the wheel so she could sit back and relax, or at least try to relax. Her brain was going a lot faster than she could keep up with.

Should she quit her job? She had gone to school for eight years to have the ability to have this job. She didn't want to quit.

Was that selfish? Was it prideful? It really wasn't for her own self-interest, although she did have to do something to make a

living and to support the three girls who were coming. Except...
James could do that with his business.

Who said that she had to keep working?

They were quiet for five minutes as James drove slowly and
confidently back toward their house.

"I'm so sorry about that," she said, wondering if his silence meant
anger. He had every right to be angry with her. She most likely
would be angry with him, if he had interrupted their wedding
evening in order to take care of some kind of emergency with his
business. Even if his business was life and death, she would have a
hard time accepting it.

"You don't have to apologize. I told you that."

"But I wasn't sure you meant it. I thought you might be angry
with me. I have to admit that I might be angry with you if our
positions were reversed."

"Why would I be angry? You just saved that horse's life."

"Because it's our wedding night? You were expecting to have an
evening together with me. And I ruined it by putting on work
clothes and going off to do something with the horse. You have
every right to be upset."

"No, I don't. We talked about it. I told you to go ahead and answer
the phone. Even knowing that we would probably not make it
home until after dark."

And that had been accurate since dusk was wearing off into deep
night.

"I know. I just feel...guilty."

"Don't," he said firmly, then his hand came down and covered
hers which was sitting on her leg. He threaded his fingers with hers,
and he set them on the console between the two seats. "Thanks for
letting me come. I enjoyed watching you."

"I'm sure you have other things you'd rather have done this
evening."

"I told you not to do that," he said, a little warning in his voice.

It made her smile. "But I appreciated having you there. It was so nice to have someone helping me, and you did it just perfectly. Not too pushy, but you didn't lose interest and walk away either. I... I could get used to that."

"Then consider me your new right-hand man. I'll give you my bill."

She laughed, knowing he was joking but appreciating his easy-going attitude.

"I told you, being a businessman wasn't exactly my dream. It was more my dad's dream. He's retired, and I did my duty by him. I don't feel like I owe him anymore. I'm free. Free to continue in business, or free to start a new chapter in my life. I... I believe I have chosen to start a new chapter."

"That's what this is. Our marriage is a new chapter. But it doesn't have to be you giving up everything and me giving up nothing. I don't like that."

"I wouldn't like that either. But that's not what it is. It's us deciding together what we're going to do. I'll probably have to make a few more trips back to Chicago, but I'll unload the company. It won't be a quick process, and it won't be easy, but I'll make a nice chunk of change, and then I'll be free to be a husband, dad, and, apparently, veterinary assistant."

"And a farmer and rancher."

"Yes, that too."

Chapter 16

James pulled the SUV to a stop in front of the house. Mabel sat in the passenger seat, glad that he took the time to reassure her that he understood that being called out was part of her job. Thrilled that she had married someone who didn't want to see an animal die more than he wanted to have what he felt he deserved. An uninterrupted wedding evening.

Regardless, she wanted to make it up to him a little bit, so she said, "I think we both need to shower, and then... Are you hungry?"

She was starved, although she didn't know how much she would be able to eat because she was nervous about getting the girls in the morning.

"I'm pretty much always hungry. You can just assume the answer to that question is a yes, unless I'm unconscious."

She looked over and smiled, so happy that he wasn't angry with her. She tucked that information away in her head so she could bring it out when he did something that upset her, and she hoped she could handle it with as much grace as he had handled this evening.

"You know, you were saying back there about being upset that it was our wedding evening and everything, and expecting me to be angry or whatever. But, you know, watching you work, I'm proud of you. You're competent and know what you're doing and compassionate while still being businesslike and not wishy-washy or touchy-feely. You know? You're just the perfect balance of everything, and it made me feel good to be able to be beside you and to not just know you but to be married to you."

His words touched the spot deep in her heart, the one she didn't even know needed that reassurance.

Maybe because her parents had always been too busy, or maybe because she lost them young. Or maybe it was just a need she had, but she appreciated the validation from James. Not just that he admired her, but that he was proud of her.

It helped her to believe that he meant what he said when he said that he didn't mind at all. It was obvious he wasn't angry.

"Thank you," she said, looking across the seat at him.

"All right. I agree with you that we both need showers," he said, grabbing the door latch and getting out.

She got out as well, and they walked in the house together, putting her things where she typically kept them in the mudroom, along with her shoes which weren't dirty since she'd washed them off before they left. They were the ones that she reserved for vet calls.

Thankfully the old farmhouse had two full baths, and they were both able to shower and be back down in the kitchen in less than fifteen minutes.

Maybe she should have taken more time since it was her wedding night after all, but she would rather spend the time with him than getting ready for him. Hopefully he felt the same way.

So her hair was wet and tied loosely behind her since she was planning on cooking. And she just wore simple jeans and a T-shirt.

He came down dressed very much the same, although his hair was not long enough to put in a ponytail.

"I thought I would make us some eggs. Is that okay with you?" She hoped he didn't want anything fancier than that. She didn't think she could do it.

"All right. I'll make toast," he said, walking toward the drawer where they kept the bread.

She wished she would have asked him to make the eggs, because she was pretty sure she could make toast without burning it. Eggs, she wasn't so sure about.

But she reached into the refrigerator and pulled the carton out.

"How would you like them?" she asked, then kicking herself for it. She should have just made scrambled eggs. She could probably do scrambled.

"Over easy is my favorite, but I'll take them however you do them."

"Over easy it is," she said, hoping that the confidence she infused in her voice would show up in her actions as well since she'd never made eggs over easy in her life before.

She wasn't even sure she could crack them without breaking the yolk.

"What do you think about getting our own chickens?" James asked as he pulled two pieces of bread out of the bag.

"I think that would be pretty awesome. I think the girls would love it too. Although, I assume that you would probably be taking care of them, right?"

She wasn't sure. He had talked about being a stay-at-home dad, taking care of the girls, letting the business go. But they hadn't made any firm decisions as far as she could tell.

"Actually, I wanted to talk to you about that. I mean, yes, I would think that I would be taking care of pretty much everything around the house if we agree that I'll sell the business and be here permanently, supporting you and raising our kids. I mean, I might dabble in a few things online, but nothing that would take me away from all of you."

She wasn't quite sure exactly what he thought he was going to get into online, but because of his talent in business, she figured it would probably be something profitable.

"I just don't want you to feel trapped here. I don't want you to feel like you're stuck. Or that you hate it and you want to do something else."

"All right. I'll keep that in mind. I guess I've never been home raising children, and I've never been on a farm before taking care of it for any length of time. But I have to admit I'm excited about all of it. I want to get started."

"Tomorrow. I'm a little nervous."

"I am too. But I'm just as excited as I am nervous."

"That's true for me too. I can't wait to be a family. I can't wait to get started doing the family things."

"Doing family farm things. Having chickens, maybe getting a few other animals... Would that be okay?"

"As much as you want. I'm down for whatever." She cracked the first egg in the bowl and didn't break the yolk. What were the odds that she could do all four like that?

"There's some bacon in the fridge. Do you want me to fry that up too?"

"Sure. I guess it'll be up to us to do the grocery shopping. Maybe we should figure some of that stuff out?"

"I was thinking we should sit down with Aunt Carol and hash out the things that we're doing. I told her she didn't have to pay rent, because she was doing me a favor by living in my house and taking care of it. I know she loves to cook, and I know you don't, so it probably wouldn't be a hardship for you to give that up to either Aunt Carol or me, but maybe we can hash some of those things out at some point."

"I think that's a great idea. I don't know how things will go tomorrow, but maybe after the girls go to bed, we can talk about it?"

"Sometime. Someday this week when the girls go to bed and we're all there, or... Maybe the girls should sit with us while we talk about it if they want to."

She liked that idea. Liked the thought that they would include the girls in their decision-making. "I think that would help the girls feel like they have more control over their life. If we take their opinions into account when we're making decisions. I'm glad you thought of that."

They shared a smile across the kitchen as she waited for the butter in the skillet to melt before she put the eggs in.

"I haven't met them yet, so I think maybe we'll need to play everything by ear, but I would like for them to have as much to do with the general running of the farm business as we can. I know I didn't always appreciate my dad dragging me into the business and hauling me along on work trips and that type of thing, but I never doubted that he valued my opinion and that he wanted me to be with him. Looking back, those are the things he did that probably contributed to me being in his business even though I really didn't want to. He had treated me like a part of it for so long, it felt like it was almost as much mine as it was his."

Mabel had poured the eggs in and took the bowl over to the sink, rinsing it out and setting it in the dishwasher. "Maybe that was the difference between your parents and mine. My dad dragged me along, but I felt like it was more because he didn't think I was good enough the way I was, and he wanted to change me. We never talked about his business, and he definitely never asked my opinion on anything. I didn't feel like I was part of it, I just felt like I was...an embarrassment to him."

"You couldn't possibly have been. I know for sure when I saw you there, you were not an embarrassment, you were an asset. Maybe he wanted to show you off. It certainly worked that way with me."

"I can't believe you even remember seeing me, let alone liked me. That blows my mind."

"Good. I was afraid it would seem stalkerish, and I really hesitated to tell you."

"It was hugely flattering, and while I can't believe you did, it's definitely made me see things a little bit differently. Maybe you're right. Maybe Dad really did just want to show me off."

It was hard for her to believe that, but she supposed it could be true.

"Whatever it was, I think your dad was more successful in making you believe that he wanted you. I really want to do that with our girls too. Because I think you're right. Having them think that they're an important part of our family will go a lot further toward solidifying our family, making it strong."

The toast popped up, and he turned from the bacon in the skillet to grab it and put it on the plate.

"I'm glad we agree on this. I think a lot of times people disagree on child raising, and it causes contention." He paused, the piece of toast still in his hand as he stared at it, then he looked across the kitchen at her. "Do you want more children?"

There was a little bit of uncertainty in his voice, and there was also that undercurrent of heat or attraction or whatever it was that made her spine tingle and her toes curl.

"Do you?"

"I think so. I... I could live without them. Three girls is going to be hectic enough. But I wouldn't mind having a couple more. Maybe some boys."

"You can put your order in, but I'm not sure that will work. I think typically we get what God thinks we need rather than what we want."

"I'll take whatever. Unless you don't want any?"

"I do. But I didn't want to insist on it, because a lot of people think three kids is too many. I can't imagine having four or five or more."

"I think it would be fun. I think a big family, with lots of love and laughter and friendship and craziness, would be pretty awesome. But maybe I'm just looking at it through rose-colored glasses and maybe it would be more work than what it's worth."

"I don't know, that sounds pretty fun to me. I guess... I guess as long as you're with me, I'll raise as many kids as you want to. I just don't want to do it by myself."

"As long as I'm alive, you won't be by yourself."

"I know. That was what the marriage was about today, wasn't it? And yet, I'm so used to being on my own. Or, you know, I've always had Lark, I've always had my sister, Gladys, but I don't know. I've never had a partner. I feel like I have one now. It's taken me a little bit of time to get used to the idea, but I like that feeling." And everything he said made her feel like he was actually going to stay. That he wasn't going to leave her in the lurch or duck out when things got hard.

"I guess I've heard of a few people who had a bunch of kids, and then the husband walked out on them. I always felt so bad for them. Like, you don't have five kids, or seven kids, and think you're going to raise them by yourself, you know?"

"Yeah. I guess I don't know what to say that will make you believe me when I say that I'll be here."

"I believe you, because you've done everything else you said you were going to do. But I suppose there are no guarantees in life, you know?"

She'd been so busy thinking about kids and businesses and her dad and everything that the smell of something burning hadn't registered right away.

"Oh my goodness. I think I burnt the eggs!"

She grabbed the skillet and pulled it off the burner. Smoke poured out from underneath the eggs, which were runny on top, but as she used a spatula to peel them away from the bottom, they were burnt black underneath.

"I should have just admitted to you to begin with," she said, disgusted with herself as she scraped the eggs into the garbage can. "I've never cooked eggs. Anything but scrambled. I've never done sunny side up, nor over easy, and I was just hoping I was able to do it without breaking them."

She didn't realize until her voice broke on that last sentence that tears were pooling in her eyes, and they spilled over, running down her cheeks. She'd ruined her wedding evening by going on a call; now she ruined her wedding supper by burning it. He was going to think he married the most incompetent woman in the world.

She used a spatula to scrape at the skillet where the eggs had stuck in the middle, using her sleeve to swipe her eyes and sniffing so her nose wasn't running everywhere.

"Hey," he said softly, right beside her ear before his arms went around her, and he pulled her back against him with one hand while he grabbed a hold of the skillet handle with the other. "Let me have that," he said gently, and she let go.

He set it on the sink and pulled the spatula from her hand as well before he wrapped both arms around her and cradled her there against his chest.

She turned so her cheek snuggled up against him, and she wrapped her arms around him, trying to stifle her tears. Now she was ruining everything even more by crying.

"I feel like I can't do anything right," she finally said softly against his chest, getting her tears under control but still sniffling.

"You do a lot of things right, and no one expects you to be perfect. And I kinda like that there's something that you can't do that I can. You're not going to be upset if I cook the eggs?"

"I think I can manage to butter the bread without doing anything terrible, although I'm sure I'll probably drop at least one piece."

"And it will land butter side down because it always does." She could feel him smiling over her head.

"Are you going to laugh at everything I do? Aren't you ever going to get angry?"

"I hope not. I don't ever want to be angry with you. I don't think you would ever do anything on purpose to make me angry, and even then, I'd really rather love you than be angry with you."

She froze. He said he'd rather love her.

Love.

"Hey. I need to turn the bacon, or it's going to end up like the eggs, and then it will be a true catastrophe, because burning bacon is a federal crime, whereas burning eggs is just a misdemeanor."

She laughed and backed up so he could grab the spatula. It was like he hadn't said the L word at all.

She didn't want to talk about that. Not now. Everything just felt too...too much. She didn't feel like she was good enough for any of it, and she didn't want to feel even less worthy, to have this man who seemed to do everything right loving her too.

It would just make her feel even more like she wasn't enough.

"You know," James said as he casually opened the egg carton he'd gotten out of the refrigerator and cracked an egg. "You said you keep ruining things. That you don't feel like you're good enough. You know that you are good enough, just because God loves you. That's where your worth is."

She moved to the toaster, grabbing the toast that popped up sometime during her crying spell. "I know. I guess... I just have trouble believing it."

"Don't think that you have trouble believing. Just believe. Say to yourself, God loves me, and that's where my worth is. God thinks I'm special enough to die for, and that is where my worth is. God calls me His child, and that's what makes me worthy. It has nothing to do with what you do, what you say, who you are, although as a child of God, of course we're always trying to do things that please Him. We want to. That's our goal, because He's done so much for us, but He accepts us however we are. It's our heart He looks at."

She listened quietly, knowing he was right, knowing she needed to hear these words. Because so much of what she had felt lately had been along the lines of her not being good enough.

"Maybe it's harder when we have parents that we feel like we could never please, that we could never be good enough for, which kind of translates over into feeling like we can never be good enough for God. You know? Maybe that's one of the reasons why I want to include our children in our decision-making and let them know that they're important to us. Not only do I think that will help them learn to make good decisions, but it will let them know that we value their opinion and make them feel valuable."

"I want that for them."

"Me too. But I want it for you as well. I want you to be able to see that whether you're a vet, or whether you're a stay-at-home mom. Whether you have a big, fancy degree after your name, or whether you have nothing, not even a high school diploma. It doesn't matter. Not in God's eyes. That He loves you no matter what. No matter whether you can cook eggs or not. Whether you go out on a call or whether you don't. Whether people give you accolades or whether they don't. You can stand in a corner and know you're worthy, just because you're standing under the love of your heavenly Father."

Mabel finished buttering a piece of toast, setting it on a plate, then she set her knife down and took two steps to where James stood at the stove, watching the bacon and eggs and not burning either one.

He was right.

She wrapped her arms around him and laid her head against his back. "Thank you for taking the time to make sure that I knew that. You... You might have to remind me. I know I'm going to need to remind myself too, especially when things happen that make me feel like I'm not enough."

"Because you are enough," he said, putting one of his hands over hers and using his other hand to flip the eggs. Perfectly, without breaking any of them.

She admired that.

They stood like that for a while, until her pieces of toast popped up, and she went over to butter them. Maybe this was what the rest of their marriage would be. For the rest of her life, she would have someone who reminded her of the truth when she forgot or when she knew it but wasn't able to put it into practice in her life.

She appreciated having someone like that beside her.

With that thought, she realized that she wanted to be that person for him too. Maybe he didn't need her, but that didn't mean that she couldn't be ready in case there was some time, even in the far distant future, where he did.

When everything was ready, they carried the food to the table.

He sat at the head, and she sat to his right, and he prayed without comment before they started to eat.

It was a short prayer, but she was glad of it, glad that they were starting their marriage with a prayer for God's blessing. She felt like they needed Him. Needed God's blessing not just in their marriage but in their lives.

It was late by the time they finished and did the dishes, although they sat out on the porch swing for several hours, just talking about their day and how much they had enjoyed it. Glad that they hadn't done a lot of stressful things that might have made the day more beautiful but also more difficult.

It was late when they went in and walked to the top of the stairs together. He leaned over, kissing her forehead and whispering good night, before she walked to her room.

She could feel his eyes on her back as she walked, and while she felt like it was too soon for her to move into his room tonight, she wondered what he would say if she suggested that very thing.

She kind of wanted to. But she didn't. She stopped at the door, turned and waved, and then stepped in and closed the door behind her.

Chapter 17

I t was not quite light the next day when James rolled over in bed.

He was smiling. He was married to Mabel. A dream come true. Yesterday had been the best day of his life. So far. He definitely expected more days just like that.

Although, of course he wasn't so naïve as to believe that there wouldn't be hard days as well. Of course there would be.

He was lying in bed, thinking about that, and not really wanting to get up and face the day, wanting to lie in bed and savor the memories, when he thought he heard a vehicle.

Was that what that sound was? Still a little groggy from sleep, it took him a few minutes to realize that it was indeed the sound of a motor running.

Odd. It wasn't even daylight which was rather early for a visitor. Especially anyone from town who knew that they had gotten married the day before and surely wouldn't expect them to be up before dawn.

It would have to be someone who didn't know that they had gotten married, someone with an emergency, or someone who didn't belong.

It was that last thought that made him throw back the covers and jump out of bed.

It only took a minute or two for him to put his pants and shirt on, then he grabbed socks and padded out the door.

He didn't want to wake Mabel, particularly if the person was up to no good. He didn't want to scare her.

So, he crept slowly down the stairs. Later, he wished he would have gone faster, because by the time he got to the bottom and looked out the window, all he could see were taillights and what looked like a dark SUV disappearing down the drive.

Feeling like if someone had taken a wrong turn, they wouldn't have come the whole way to the house to turn around, he headed to the back door and looked out the window.

The sun was just poking over the horizon, and the world was bathed in orange glow.

At first, he didn't see anything, but as his eyes swept back over the yard and went toward the driveway, he saw a lump.

It looked brown, but that could have been because it was in shadow. As he stared, the lump moved, and that's when he realized it was alive.

That jolted him into action, and he ran to the mudroom to put his boots on and head outside, his mind spinning. What could it be?

The girls were supposed to arrive that day, but while his rational brain said that a brown lump would not be three girls, he couldn't help but wonder if maybe whoever was bringing them would just dump them off.

The idea made him angry, and he fumbled with his boots.

Finally, he jammed his feet in them, and he yanked at the door handle, ripping the door open and striding outside.

After two fast steps, he reminded himself to go slow. He didn't think there was any danger, but something had definitely happened, and he didn't want to step into some kind of problem. More because he didn't want Mabel to get up on the day after their wedding and find him in some kind of predicament, or worse.

His eyes swept all around, trying to see if there was anything else unusual, as he made his way toward the spot where he'd seen the lump.

Nothing popped out at him, and by the time he'd gotten to the spot, a head emerged from the dark shadows, and he was pretty sure that it was a small horse. A foal. One that was very young.

"Hey there," he said softly as he approached it. Mabel was the one with all the experience with animals; he wasn't sure what to do to not scare it. Luckily, he must have done the right thing, since it didn't move when he reached it, first running his hand up its broad forehead and then rubbing between its ears.

He didn't know much, but he was almost certain that it was a newborn. Maybe up to a week old? He wasn't sure.

After looking around once more and taking a few steps around the yard, just to be sure, he decided that there was no danger, and he could run up and get Mabel.

This probably had nothing to do with the girls, nothing to do with her marriage, and everything to do with the fact that Mabel was a vet. Whatever was up with the foal, it didn't seem to be able to stand up, and Mabel was going to need to do something about that. He could cook eggs, but he couldn't diagnose a foal.

On that thought, he hurried into the house, taking the steps two at a time and striding down the hall to Mabel's room.

He could have just called her, but he hadn't thought of that until he was at her room with his hand raised to knock.

She was probably used to getting woken up at odd hours by her phone, perhaps a knock would upset her, but he didn't stop to wonder about it but rapped on her door.

She answered immediately, sounding groggy. "Yes?"

"It's James. Someone just dropped off a foal. It's in a heap outside."

"I'll be right there," she said immediately, sounding much more awake than she had with her first word.

He wanted to wait for her but wasn't sure whether that would be entirely appropriate, and he couldn't get himself to stand still anyway. His heart was racing, and he felt like he was close to panic, and he wanted to talk to Mabel. Pretty sure she could talk him off the ledge. She would look at the foal, she would know what to do, and then she would start to plan. All he had to do was wait for her.

Deciding that his time would be put to best use by going out and checking once more to make sure that nothing else had been dropped off, he hurried back outside and made a sweep of the yard. Just in the few minutes that he'd been inside, it had gotten noticeably brighter, and he could tell that there was nothing else around.

It was less than five minutes when Mabel stepped outside.

"James! Where is it?" she asked immediately as her eyes landed on him.

He hurried toward her, pointing back to where the foal still lay on the ground.

"Oh my goodness," she said, hurrying toward it. "It's still alive!" she said as she got close enough to see it move.

"Yeah. But I haven't seen it stand up."

"Did you talk to the person who dropped it off? Did they say what was wrong with it? Did they give you any idea how old or what the situation is?"

"No to everything. I heard a motor, got dressed, and came out, and all I saw was taillights when I got downstairs. Maybe a dark SUV, but I didn't see any note, didn't see anything else other than this little guy lying right here."

She was already kneeling beside the baby, and after lifting a leg, she said, "It's a little girl."

"All right. That's good to know."

"I guess we're going to assume that this little girl either had her mom die, or her mom didn't have enough milk for her, or something happened to her. Maybe her mom rejected her. Possibly she's a twin, but she looks too big for that." She talked a little more about what breed she might be, engaged in some speculation, all the while she took her temperature, checked her eyes, ran her hands over her body, and did all the things that he would never have thought to do.

"All right. I think the first thing I'm going to need to do is get some formula. I don't have any foal milk replacer, but I know people who do. I'm going to send a couple of texts and ask if I can borrow some, then I'm going to send you a link, and you can order some for me. My wallet is in my purse hanging on the hook inside the door. You can use my card to pay for it."

"I think I can pay for it," he said, pulling out his phone. "I'm ready whenever you send it."

"All right." That's all she said as her fingers flew over the phone.

Less than twenty minutes later, someone dropped off foal milk replacer, and Mabel had it mixed up and ready.

James supposed he shouldn't be surprised to see a neighbor was not only up but answering their phone and ready to do a good deed. It made him appreciate his rural area as he stood with Mabel by the sink.

"Aren't you going to put it in a bottle?" James said as he followed her back out to the foal, carrying the bucket of milk replacer for her.

"A lot of times, a foal won't take artificial nipples, because we really don't have anything that mimics her mom very well at all. But even a very young foal will drink from a bucket. We'll try this first, and if it doesn't work, I'll need to go to Lark's and grab a bottle since I don't have one here."

"I see."

"Now, I'm hoping that we're going to be able to get her to stand. I'm going to show you what I need you to do."

"All right," James said, setting the bucket down and standing beside Mabel so she could give him instructions.

"Horses get up by stretching their front feet out in front of them, and they put a lot of their strength on their front end, until they get their hind underneath them, and then they push up. So, I'll

be working to mimic that with her and stretch her front legs out."
She did that while she talked, and then she said, "Now, ideally, if I
come back here to her rear and just push a little bit on it, lifting up
some, she will hopefully get the idea and give me a hand, pushing
up with her legs."

"All right."

"Now, what I'm going to ask you to do is to keep your eye on
her. If she looks like she's wobbly, see if you can help her balance.
Maybe by putting one hand on both sides and just keeping her
from tumbling over. If it looks like she can't quite hold her own
weight, maybe you could put a hand under her and give her a hand
with that. We can feed her while she's lying down, but I would
prefer for her to be standing up. It will be less messy."

He didn't ask questions but positioned himself beside her front
shoulders and stood there while Mabel worked on the rear end.

It worked just like she said, even better, since once the filly was
up, it took her a couple of moments to balance, and then she gave
a soft whinny and took a step.

"That's better than I thought," Mabel said with relief in her tone
as her eyes tracked the foal. "But she is extremely skinny, and depending on her nutrition level, and whether she got any colostrum
or not, there are a variety of problems that can crop up in the next
few days to a week."

"That would stink. Serious things?"

"Yes. If a horse gets an infection in their joints, which is one of
the things that can happen, you almost always have to put them
down, because they're not really good for anything, and they won't
have a nice life."

As she talked, she had gotten the bucket and dipped her fingers
in it, rubbing them over the filly's nose.

"She smells it. And look, she has her tongue out. She's tasting it."
She giggled a little at the sweet little antics of the filly. "I put some
corn syrup in it because that sweetens it just a little bit."

"Horses have a sweet tooth?"

"They do. Even young ones like this. It just makes them hopeful-ly want to eat as much as they can, and as I suspected, she definitely needs as many calories as we can pump into her."

Within a couple of minutes, Mabel had the little filly's nose in the bucket, and she was slurping the milk down.

"She drank it all," he said, surprised.

"Yeah. I wasn't expecting that either. But I just made a quarter of a bottle. It's better to give them lots of small meals than it is to give them a couple of big ones. So, every two hours we're going to need to give her that much, and once she's done that for twenty-four hours, or maybe even thirty-six, we'll bump it up."

"Through the night?" he asked, thinking that someone was going to have to get up every two hours.

"Yeah. Raising babies is not for the faint of heart."

"Or for people who like to sleep apparently," he couldn't keep from saying.

She gave him a weary smile. "That too. For a while anyway."

"How long?"

"For the first couple of weeks, and it should be every two hours around the clock. Then, you can probably back it off to every three or four hours at night, but I'd keep it every two or three hours during the day. Especially if she's not thriving. If she's thriving, that's a different story, and you might be able to bump up the meals and do it less often. Still, if you want the very best outcome, frequent smaller meals is the best."

"And then?" he asked, still trying to figure out whether they were going to be doing this for years, or for a couple of weeks, or till Christmas.

"By the time she's a month old, you could probably be doing it every six hours and longer overnight. But," she smiled at him, "if she can get up on her own, you can leave some milk out overnight, so even when she's two or three weeks, she can go to her bucket and feed herself. That would be the key."

"I see."

"Still, the absolute best thing to do would be to feed her fresh milk mixed up every two to three hours."

"Spoken like a vet."

"Right? In a couple of days, if she's still with us, and we're getting up every two hours, I think we'll all be more than willing to back it off a little and just give her some milk that she can eat herself in a bucket."

He laughed, but he caught her words, *if she's still with us*. "Do you think she's gonna make it?"

Mabel's smile faded slowly from her face as she looked at the little filly, who had taken two steps and then lain down. She flopped more than lay, since her legs seemed to be too weak to lower herself gently to the ground.

"I don't know. Babies are touchy, and when they go down, it's awfully hard to get them back up. And they fade fast."

He nodded, still not entirely sure of what exactly she thought, but understanding that it would be touch and go, and she probably couldn't say for sure whether the filly had a good shot or not.

"Well, we talked yesterday about getting some animals. Here's our first one." He shook his head. "I can't believe someone just dropped her off. Do you think they'll be back for her?"

"You know, people do this at farms, all the time. I'll have farmers bringing an animal in to me and say someone just dropped it off in the driveway, and sometimes they take care of it, paying for it, and sometimes they want me to take it in."

"We can't take every animal that you're given."

"No. Farmers really can't either. It's not fair. But you do what you can. And you never turn humans away."

She smiled, looking up in his eyes, and he understood that. And appreciated it. That she differentiated between the idea that humans were different from animals. Humans were made in the image of God, with an eternal spirit.

Animals were part of the created world that man was given dominion over.

There was a clear differentiation in God's Word and in God's eyes.

Speaking of humans, he remembered about the girls and checked his watch. "Our girls should be here any minute."

"Wow. The morning is flying by," Mabel said, bending down and giving the filly one last pat on the head. "Maybe, the first thing they can do once they get here is name our new baby. Kind of funny that everybody's arriving on the same day."

"Sure is. But I guess that makes it more special," James said, looking at the filly once more, wondering who would just drop her off. But he supposed if they didn't have the resources to care for her or possibly the money to pay for her care, they did the best thing they could.

It put the burden on Mabel, which annoyed him a bit, because she already had enough on her plate, but he also knew that she didn't mind. And she would do her best to help. He was almost positive if he would ask, she would say that she would rather they drop it off for her to take care of it than allow it to be neglected and die without care.

He had his hand on the door to open it for Mabel when the sound of a car motor had them both stopping and looking at the driveway.

"Looks like they're here," he said, his stomach churning now that the time was actually here. Would they like him? Would they accept him? They already liked Mabel. She'd spent time with them before. What about him? Would they resent the fact that there was a man in the picture now?

Maybe they should have waited to get married.

He tried not to second-guess too much, but so much was riding on everything, and it felt like a wrong decision could get everything started on the wrong foot.

But the decisions had been made, and he couldn't change them, so he pointed his face forward, and opening the door, he waited for Mabel to set the bucket inside, then she straightened and came back and stood beside him.

Now was the moment of truth.

Chapter 18

Mabel stood beside James, scared, nervous, and excited too. She'd been thrilled about the filly that had shown up, although sad as well. And also, she was under no illusions about how much work it was going to be. Feeding every two hours didn't sound like much, until one realized that it was going to take thirty to forty-five minutes to mix the formula, get the baby up, feed her, making sure she ate as much as possible, and then make sure when she lay back down she didn't crumble into a heap that would hurt herself.

So it was like forty-five minutes of work every two hours, which she wasn't quite sure how she was going to fit that in with her job and with the three girls. James would help, and he'd watched everything she'd done with an eagle eye. He had been such a huge help the day before, and now today was the same. She felt like it wouldn't be just her, but even if they split the time, it was still a lot.

Still, it would be worth it if they could save the foal's life.

And if the girls loved horses, it would be even better.

The car pulled to a stop, and Mabel couldn't stand and wait for the kids to get out. She walked to the passenger side front door, where she could see a head through the windshield. It looked like Annabelle, the oldest. One of the neat things that the girls' mother had done was when she named the girls, she had done it in alphabetical order, so Annabelle was the oldest at eleven, Bernice was second at nine, and Caren was third at seven.

Annabelle burst from the car and ran to Mabel, wrapping her arms around her and squeezing hard.

Her action eased Mabel's anxiety considerably. The girls had seemed to love her when they had been there before, but it had been a long time, and she wasn't sure how they would feel with this more permanent move.

"I missed you so much, Annabelle. Look at how you've grown!"

"Grandma says I've grown out of all my clothes, and since I can't wear hand-me-downs, she is going to give me a gunnysack to put on. Whatever that is. But I don't think our school dress code will let me wear that."

"Well, if you have to wear gunnysacks, I'll wear them too, so we'll match." Mabel said as she stood back, looking at Annabelle's bright eyes and excited face.

"Grandma said we're going to stay here forever. Is that true?" she asked, as though she couldn't really believe it.

"That's true. Your grandma wouldn't lie to you."

"Yes, she would," Annabelle said, her face dropping.

"All right. I would not lie to you, and you have a home with me forever," she said with confidence, brushing over the painful truth that her grandma had lied to her.

Of course, there were times when an adult was physically incapable of keeping their word. Sometimes things came up that they just couldn't anticipate, and kids sometimes were very harsh in their judgments.

Mabel knew all of this from the teenagers that she'd helped Lark to raise, but still... It was sad to hear a child say that she couldn't trust her grandma to tell her the truth.

"Miss Mabel!" Caren said as she popped out of the back of the car and came running to Mabel, hugging her the same way Annabelle had.

Bernice was always the one who hung back a little; she was a bit more shy and more reticent than her more outgoing sisters. She was the serious one and the one who reminded Mabel the most of herself, since she was quiet but thoughtful and seemed to take everything in with her big brown eyes.

She hugged Caren and waited for Bernice to come around the car. Even Bernice's usually stoic features were shining, although her movements were not nearly as quick and excited as her siblings.

"Bernice! It's so good to see you too. Can you give me a hug?"

Bernice was not nearly as demonstrative either. Mabel knew she wasn't allowed to have favorites with her children, but if she were, Bernice would be the one, just because she seemed to need a little bit extra, even though she was the one who seemed to be the most self-sufficient and independent.

Maybe it was because Mabel could see so much of herself in her.

"So this is the man you married," Janice said as she got slowly out of the car.

She was not quite sixty, but she looked ten years older. A hard life would do that to a person, and Mabel felt bad for her and grateful as well, that she was willing to do a good thing for the girls. Although, she had acted like they were more of a nuisance to her than anything. So maybe she was just happy to get rid of them. Mabel wasn't sure.

Then her words registered, and Mabel remembered James, her husband.

"Oh my goodness, girls. I forgot all about Mr. James. I got married yesterday. And this is my husband. He's going to be living with us as well, of course, and if you feel like you want, he'll be your dad."

She kinda stumbled a little. Because the girls had never actually had a father that she knew of. They'd never called anyone dad. James wouldn't be stepping on anyone's toes, but a parent could be a touchy thing, and not every child was eager to give an adult a name that meant so much.

Mabel might be wrong, but she figured Bernice was probably the one that would be the slowest to accept him.

As she figured, Bernice hung back as Mabel turned slightly toward James and introduced them.

"Hey there, girls. Mabel told me so much about you, and I have to admit I'm nervous, because I want you to like me."

James admitting that right off seemed to melt Annabelle's heart, and she said, "I'm sure we're going to like you. Miss Mabel married you, so you must be pretty special. I didn't know that she was ever going to get married. I thought she'd just be a vet all of her life and never have a boyfriend. Let alone a husband."

Annabelle always said whatever was on her mind. She was the most outspoken of the girls.

James grinned. "I guess I'm one lucky fella then, since she not only decided she wanted a boyfriend, she decided she wanted a husband."

"And you've been an excellent husband," Mabel had to add.

James looked up, gratitude in his eyes, that she would give her stamp of approval to him, to help ease the way and encourage the girls to like him as she did, even if it had only been a day.

"Is this your house?" Caren asked, looking up at the big white house beside them.

"It's actually James's house," Mabel said, hoping that would endear him to them even more.

"That worked out pretty well for you. Marry the man and get a house," Janice said, and her comment sounded a little bit snide. Not that she was jealous, but just that sometimes life seemed to work out for some people and not for others. Mabel was sure that was true, but sometimes life worked out because you worked hard at making it work out.

And sometimes it didn't work out because a person made bad choices that they couldn't recover from.

Sometimes people were just handed a bad deck. Still, the point of life was not to win, necessarily, but to make the best of what a person had been given.

There was no point in getting into a discussion with Janice about it though, so she said, "I got the whole package," and she smiled.

James chuckled, not seeming offended at all. She really didn't think he would be. He knew she hadn't married him for his money or for his house.

Although, she supposed a less secure man might be concerned about that.

The girls chattered as Janice went to the back of the car and got suitcases and boxes out of it.

"I didn't bring their beds or anything. I figured you wouldn't need them, but if you do, you can hire a moving company to come get them. Just let me know, and I won't donate them to charity, or sell them, or whatever. I can't move them, so there was no point in even trying."

A suitcase, the ends fraying, looking like it was as old as Methuselah, slapped down on the gravel before she reached for another one.

The girls asked questions faster than Mabel could keep up with them, and she didn't try to answer Janice, other than to say, "I don't think we need beds." She looked at James to confirm her words.

He nodded, confirming she was correct.

Janice shrugged and rattled off some instructions, letting Mabel know where they stood with custody and the option for adoption. Thankful that Janice was not going to give her any trouble as she worked on adopting the girls, she nodded her head and listened to the things that Janice had set in motion.

"What's that?" A voice cut into Janice's monologue, making Mabel's head jerk.

"That's a foal that someone dropped off here this morning. Since Miss Mabel was a vet, I guess they figured she would know what to do with it."

"It belongs to you?" Annabelle said, disbelief lacing every word of her little squeaky voice.

"Us. It belongs to us," James corrected her, making Mabel smile.

Janice looked at the girls, almost glaring at them, then almost begrudgingly, she said, "They're really going to love it here, aren't they?"

Mabel smiled. "I'm so glad you had the stipulation that you wanted them to have a father. I... I wouldn't have gotten married without it. And yes. I think they're going to absolutely love it here."

"So what, did you just pick him up off the street?" Janice asked as she slammed her trunk closed.

"No. I've known James for a long time. He worked with my dad. But he wasn't really on my radar until I needed someone. And then he stepped up. I'll always be grateful for that."

She realized her words were true. That's exactly what James had done, and he'd done it with no hesitation and no conditions. Just was there when she needed him.

She watched the girls as James showed them how to stroke the filly's face and pet between her ears.

The filly struggled to get up, and the girls squealed and stepped backward, but she couldn't make it to her feet and flopped back down.

The girls crept closer again, listening to James as he talked about how they had fed her that morning and how Mabel had decided she would feed her out of a bucket.

She heard the questions going a mile a minute at James and loved seeing how patient he was at answering them.

"You might have gotten yourself a good man there," Janice said, and again, it sounded like begrudging praise.

Mabel smiled easily. "I know I did."

"Some people have all the luck," Janice said, turning back to the suitcases. "There ain't a whole lot of clothes in there for Annabelle. She grew a whole lot this school year, and didn't have no money to keep buying her more clothes, so she just had to make do with what she had. You can cut the jeans off, and she can wear cutoffs all summer. That ain't gonna hurt her none. Then you can buy her clothes for fall."

"All right. Thank you. We'll take care of it."

"I know you will. Vets are rich."

"Well, I spent a lot of money on school." She had been blessed that her parents had provided some money for her schooling, and then after they died, money had come from somewhere, she wasn't even sure where. But she graduated debt-free. As far as she knew, she was the only one in her class who did.

She was definitely grateful.

"All right, girls, I'm gonna leave. I need to get back so I can open the door for the mortgage inspection," Janice hollered over to the girls, and they slowly stood, walking over to her.

Mabel wasn't sure whether their slow movements were because they were sad that Janice was leaving, or because they didn't want to leave the filly.

They halfheartedly hugged Janice as she told them to be good and told them to call her if they needed her.

It was sad for Mabel to watch. As rough as Janice pretended to be, it couldn't be an easy thing for her to walk away from her grandchildren, knowing that she was handing them over to people who wanted to adopt them and that she would lose guardianship of them completely.

At the same time, she was old enough, and perhaps in such poor health, that it must be a relief to know that they would be well taken care of.

Mabel could only imagine what she was feeling, since she didn't say, and she left without saying much more.

Mabel let the suitcases sit in the driveway where Janice had left them and walked over to where the girls had gone back to petting the filly.

"They're trying to figure out a name for it," James said as she approached him.

"I think she ought to be Rainbow," Caren said, beating the other two girls and saying her name first. Like that would sway Mabel's opinion.

"That's a dumb name. She needs to have a pretty name, like Diana."

"Diana is the name of the goddess in ancient times. People committed idolatry by worshiping her," Mabel said casually and hopefully without too much judgment. She didn't think she wanted to name an animal after a goddess, but she supposed that a name was just a name.

And there was something very regal about Diana.

"I want to call her Brownie. Because she's brown," Bernice said, shrugging her shoulders, like that was the obvious choice.

"Well, foals are really a lot different than other baby animals, and sometimes the color that they're born with isn't the color that they end up being at all. She's brown now, but she might end up being a white horse."

"Really?" James said, tilting his head like he wasn't quite sure he believed her.

"It's true. I know that's kind of crazy, but they really can totally change their looks by the time they're a year old. After that, it's not as common, but I've seen paint horses who had obvious markings on them turn completely white. And of course, dapple gray horses usually turn white as they age as well."

The girls were listening, and while Mabel figured that they weren't going to learn everything in a day, it didn't hurt to give them a little bit of information to absorb piece by piece so that they learned a little bit at a time.

Maybe that was just her hoping. It seemed like kids picked up a lot, but it had to be thrown out in order for them to pick it up.

"What do you think we should name her?" James asked.

"Well, we have Annabelle, Bernice, and Caren. Maybe we should name her something that starts with a D? After all, all four of you came on the same day."

"That's right! She's just as new as we are!" Annabelle said.

"Exactly. We thought we were getting three girls today, and we ended up with four. So, since she's the youngest, she would need the D name. But I really don't care."

"Then we could name her Diana! Because that starts with a D!"

Mabel laughed to herself. It sure did. And it was the one name she hadn't really wanted.

"But it's not fair that the name that you wanted was the name that we'll pick. Mr. James, what do you think?"

"Well, Diana does start with D, and I think it would be a good idea to pick a name that starts with D, but there is also Dana and Danielle and Denise—"

"I like Denise!"

"What about Dolly?" Bernice said.

"That's pretty."

"You guys could all pick a D name, we could stick them in a hat, and when Aunt Carol gets home, we'll have her pick out of the hat, and that way it's fair," James suggested.

"Who's Aunt Carol?" Bernice said, her eyes narrowed in suspicion, like they were going to spring something on her that she wasn't expecting and wasn't going to like.

"She's my aunt. When my mom died, when I was about your age, Aunt Carol took me when my dad couldn't watch me, and she's like a mom to me. I think you'll love her, and if you don't love her, I think you'll love her cooking. She makes really good lasagna, and a couple days ago, she made brownie cheesecake. I think there's still some left over in the kitchen somewhere."

"We haven't had breakfast yet," Caren said, sticking her bottom lip out.

"All right. I know James makes really good eggs, and I can make toast," Mabel said.

"And we can have cheesecake for dessert," Annabelle suggested hopefully.

Mabel laughed. Then she shrugged her shoulders. "That's fine with me."

It wasn't the healthiest thing the kids would ever eat, but it might be a memorable breakfast. There would be plenty of time to institute healthy eating habits, since from what Mabel knew about them, they ate mostly junk when they were with their grandmother.

"We have to feed the baby every two hours, so if we go in and eat breakfast, it'll be time to feed her again by the time we're done."

"Can I feed her?" Annabelle asked immediately.

"I'm sure you can. She eats every two hours, so there will be a turn for everyone. In fact, we can get busy making a schedule for that if you guys want to."

"I want to be on the schedule," Bernice said, and she actually sounded eager and somewhat excited.

Mabel smiled to herself, hoping that maybe Bernice would come out of her shell a little bit and not be afraid to show emotion.

She didn't think that she would ever be like her sisters, and she really didn't want her to be. Bernice needed to be Bernice, just a version of Bernice that wasn't scared that everyone was going to try to take advantage of her if she allowed them into her life and heart.

The girls stood. James picked a suitcase up in each hand and shoved one under his arm, and each of the girls picked up two as well.

With Mabel carrying two, they were able to get everything except for the bags into the house on the first trip.

Mabel couldn't complain about how the first few hours had gone. Hopefully, the rest of the girls' transition would be just as smooth.

Chapter 19

B reakfast had been over for hours, and they were busy upstairs putting the rooms together. The house had six bedrooms total, and thankfully there were beds in each of them, so they didn't need more.

James figured he would need to talk to Mabel later, but he thought they could use another dresser and some mirrors.

He figured girls were a little different than boys that way, although even as a boy, he sometimes found himself staring in the mirror.

But they had things almost situated. The girls really didn't have a whole lot of stuff, and James figured there would be a shopping trip or more in their near future.

There weren't any toys, just a couple of dolls, and very few clothes that weren't worn or torn or both.

That wasn't something he wanted to talk about in front of the girls though.

He also wanted to discuss with Mabel the things that Janice had been saying while he was talking to the girls about the filly.

They had to stop and feed the foal, and each of the girls had come up with a D name that they had written on a piece of paper, folded, and put into a hat.

When Aunt Carol arrived, they were going to have her draw a name, and each of the girls had agreed that whatever name was drawn would be the name of the filly.

The filly still wasn't getting up on her own, not for the first three feedings that they'd given her.

Mabel said it might just take a little while until she got her strength built up, but the idea that the filly couldn't get up herself worried James.

He trusted his wife and figured she knew better than he did, so he tried not to show that he was concerned. It wouldn't be good for the girls anyway.

They were about to break for lunch when they heard Aunt Carol arrive.

"Hello?" she called. "Are there some new girls in the house today?" she said as she walked in.

"Is that Aunt Carol?" Annabelle said, tilting her head and listening.

"Sure sounds like it. Let's get out of here; it's about time for lunch anyway."

The girls all ran for the stairs. He wasn't sure whether it was the mention of lunch or the fact that he'd been casually talking about Aunt Carol as they worked through the morning, mentioning what a good cook she was, telling them a few stories about things Aunt Carol had done with him when he was growing up. How he had such a good time at her house, and how she took him to the zoo and on his first airplane ride, and how they'd seen the ocean together. As well as the picnic they'd had in the backyard, and how she'd allowed him to set up a lemonade stand on the sidewalk in front of her house when he was trying to earn money to buy a pair of roller skates.

The girls had asked if they could set up a lemonade stand, and James had said he was fine with that, but that sometimes a person had to consider their location and whether or not the business they wanted to engage in would be the right fit for the area they were in.

The girls looked at him like he was crazy, and then he said, "How many cars have you seen go by our front porch since you arrived here?"

It took a little bit for the light to dawn in their eyes, but then they realized that he was saying that they wouldn't have any customers.

They looked kind of sad after that, but he said that if they put their heads to it, maybe they could figure out another business they could engage in.

Like caring for orphan foals for people who couldn't do it, Mabel suggested as they fed the filly for the fourth time.

"Hey, Aunt Carol, I found those three little girls you were talking about. They came with clothes and a couple of dolls, now they think they need to move into rooms upstairs," James said as he walked in the kitchen with the girls running around on all sides of him.

Mabel brought up the rear, and as he turned to watch her walk in the kitchen, he noted her bright, red cheeks and shining eyes, and knew she'd been having a great morning.

Lark had said that she would try to cover all the calls and that she would only call Mabel if she absolutely needed to.

James appreciated that, because he wanted Mabel to be there to settle into the family together.

He was glad about that decision, since she seemed to really enjoy the children. Maybe he was putting too much stock in things, but she seemed to really enjoy being around him, too.

They introduced the girls to Aunt Carol, and they gathered around her, asking if she really did have picnics in the backyard and lemonade stands on the front porch.

Her eyes twinkled, and she looked up at James, almost as though saying *you told my secrets*, but she smiled, and he figured that she felt the same way he did when Mabel had smoothed the way for him.

She had the girls helping her make lunch in no time at all while he and Mabel set the table.

He put his arm around her waist, and drew her to him, and said, "You look happy."

"I am. I... I never envisioned a day like today, but it's been the best of days."

"For me too. Thank you."

"I think it's me that should be thanking you. You've...created a home for us."

"We created a home together."

He wanted to add that God had brought them together, but she already knew that, and even though they weren't talking about Him, He was in the midst of them. Anywhere there was joy and laughter and kindness and consideration, God was there.

And their home seemed to be full of all the good things. He just hoped that it continued in that way, because he loved the happiness that seemed to radiate out of their home.

"I love the girls. You were right about them," he continued, pulling her closer and dropping a kiss on her temple.

She closed her eyes and smiled, and that almost made him bolder. But they had the rest of their lives, and he didn't have to rush anything today. There had been a lot of changes, and although he felt that most of them were good, he still didn't want to push Mabel into things she wasn't ready for.

"All right, lunch is on the table," Aunt Carol said as they all gathered round.

It didn't take them long to eat, although they sat and talked for a while, with the girls telling them stories about their homelife and the adults at the table trying to hide their dismay.

James kept telling himself that they were with people who loved them now and could care for them properly.

After they ate, it was time to feed the filly again, but before they went out, they handed the hat to Aunt Carol.

"We all put a D name in there, and you're going to pull one of them, and then that's going to be her name."

"All right. I am not sure I can handle this much pressure, but I'll do my best," Aunt Carol said, sticking her hand into the hat and pulling out a slip of paper. "Denise."

"Yay! You picked my name!"

"Oh, that stinks. I was hoping we could call her Dolly."

"We agreed that we were going to go with the name that came out of the hat. Denise it is," James said in a tone that brooked no argument. The girls must have understood that tone, because two of them didn't look happy, but they didn't argue anymore.

"All right, you guys can all come out, and we'll practice mixing up Denise's milk."

Mabel led the way to the mudroom, where there was a deep sink and where the bucket of milk replacer sat.

"Remember, it doesn't have to be warm, but until she's drinking really well, I like to warm it up some. She's young, and she would be getting milk from her mom, so I like to imitate that."

She reminded them how to measure the cup, and after she filled the container up to the specific amount, she shook it and then added a little bit of corn syrup.

"What's that again?" Annabelle asked, her eyes glued on everything that Mabel did.

"This is corn syrup. It makes it sweet, kind of like sugar, only sugar is a little bit hard on her little tummy, so we use corn syrup instead, which is easier for her digestion. Even though horses have a sweet tooth. This should help her drink a little bit better."

"Oh," she said, watching as Mabel put her hand over one end of the bottle and shook it up.

After the milk was ready, the girls followed Mabel out the door, with James bringing up the rear. Aunt Carol had stayed in to clean off the table.

That reminded James that he wanted to talk to his aunt and make sure that they weren't giving her more work than she could handle. If he knew her, like he thought he did, she would say that she just wanted to stay busy, and she was happy to have people to serve.

He could be wrong, but he would be shocked if she said the girls were a nuisance in any way.

They got Denise up, and immediately she put her head in the bucket and slurped all the milk they had just made down.

"She's still hungry!" Bernice said, concern on her face as Denise lifted her head and looked around.

"And we'll start feeding her a little bit more once we're sure that she's going to be okay eating this much. Probably tomorrow. And then, when she's eating even more, we won't have to feed her so often."

The girls nodded solemnly and then petted Denise.

Mabel showed them how to run their hands down her legs and lift her feet, teaching her that it was okay to have someone touching her and working with her feet.

"A horse doesn't like to have anyone touching their feet, because that is the defense mechanism that God gave them—to run away. So, if someone's holding onto their feet, they're vulnerable to an enemy or predator. So that's why, when they're young, you start working with them so that they know that allowing you to pick up their feet doesn't hurt them, and they'll be fine. That way, if you ever want to put shoes on them, or when the farrier comes just to trim their hooves, they don't get all upset about it."

"She let me pick them up!" Annabelle said as she picked up Denise's front foot.

"That's excellent. You're being very gentle. And that's what we want. We want to make sure that we don't hurt her and that she feels safe around us. That teaches her that it's okay and people are safe and won't hurt her."

James smiled at the girls' serious looks as they listened to Mabel teach them about the foal.

He wondered how much of what she said they would learn and remember, but he figured it didn't matter, even if they retained a little bit, the experience was the big thing. People had a tendency to remember what they did a lot more than they remembered what they heard, although when what they heard matched what they did, the retention rate almost assuredly went up.

They were on their way back into the house when a car pulled down the driveway.

"We have visitors," Mabel said as she looked at the car maneuvering slowly toward them.

"Let me take the bucket and bottle in, and I'll wash them out, while you guys greet them," James said, holding his hand out for the bucket.

She handed it to him, and their eyes met for a moment. Maybe she was remembering their embrace before lunch. He certainly was. He wouldn't mind repeating that and found himself looking forward to it. A little nervous at the idea that she might not want to.

He shook the thought aside as he walked in the house. He supposed they might have company all day, people wishing them well on their wedding and wanting to meet their new charges.

He might not have another private moment with his wife until after they put the kids to bed tonight.

He looked forward to it.

Chapter 20

Mabel walked to the car that had just pulled into the drive, smiling because she recognized the matchmakers from in town.

They didn't officially call themselves that, since they met at the community center to do crafts and quilting. But most people in town referred to them that way, and for good reason. They had as much of a reputation for matchmaking as Billy the Highland steer did.

Miss Helen, Miss April, and Miss June got out of their car and came over and gave her a hug, congratulating her on her wedding.

"Would you ladies like to sit on the porch?" she asked after she introduced Annabelle, Bernice, and Caren.

"Sure. Although, was that a horse in your front yard?" Miss April said as she walked with them to the porch.

"It is. Someone dropped her off this morning. She's very close to being a newborn, but we've got her eating, and I think her prognosis is guarded. As long as she makes it through the next week or so without any trouble and starts getting up on her own, I think she's going to make it." She hoped that was true. She supposed she wouldn't be quite so optimistic if it were someone else's animal. She would have to be honest and say that the odds were probably not quite fifty-fifty.

It was funny how a person could lie to themselves when they wouldn't utter a lie to someone else.

"I bet your girls loved that," Miss June said as she climbed the stairs to the front porch.

"They're doing a great job with her. I was teaching them how to feed her, and I think that probably the older two especially will be able to feed her on their own, if she continues to do well."

"There's nothing like growing up on a farm for raising kids."

Miss April and Miss June nodded at Miss Helen's words.

Mabel couldn't disagree. She was happy and grateful that James had had the foresight to buy this property, and that it had come with such a huge house. She could imagine them filling it with children over the years. The idea made her smile.

"I brought you a casserole, and if it's okay, I'll just slip in the house and put it on the counter," Miss April said, holding up the casserole that Mabel had not noticed until then.

"I'm so sorry. Yes, of course. Carol is in there, along with James, and I'm sure they can take it from you."

She opened the door and held it while Miss April walked in.

She got Miss June and Miss Helen seated, and they'd started talking about the weather when Miss April came out with Carol and James.

They all settled on seats on the porch and casually watched the children play in the yard with a ball someone had found in the shed.

"I heard something about a pistol, a matchmaking pistol. Now, are you going to tell me that Sweet Water has their own match-makers, a matchmaking steer, and now we have a matchmaking pistol?" Miss April looked from Mabel to James to Carol.

Carol looked guilty.

"Carol?" Miss April said, as though prompting her to go ahead and spill the truth.

Carol couldn't contain herself. "It's all my fault. When I was living in Oklahoma, I heard about the pistol. It belonged to Annie Oakley and was supposed to have some kind of matchmaking qualities. I knew that my nephew," she beamed at James, "had carried a torch for Mabel for years. I just had some loose idea in my head that the pistol might be able to bring them together. But the pistol always has to be passed through the woman. And I didn't know how I was going to give it to Mabel until, lo and behold, she volunteered to move in with me."

"James, you didn't have anything to do with that, did you?" Miss Helen said with a knowing gleam in her eye.

"I don't think I did. Maybe. Can I plead the fifth?" James stammered a little, which made Mabel want to laugh. She was pretty sure he didn't have anything to do with her moving in. Carol had just needed someone to live with her, and Mabel had volunteered. After all, Lark had needed the extra bedroom to house more girls, and the location wasn't far from Lark's farm, so Mabel figured that if they needed her there, it would be a short ride.

"It was an easy decision, but more because of Lark needing room at her farm than because of James."

"Oh, we all knew that you had no idea that James even existed," Miss June said, waving her hand.

Mabel gritted her teeth and looked at James. She didn't want to hurt his feelings, and she was afraid that might have, but he looked casual, like he already knew that, and the ladies weren't saying anything that he hadn't already accepted as truth. Mabel had to admit that she appreciated that.

"Anyway, the pistol supposedly has a list of the ladies who have been matched by it, and at some point, Mabel needs to add her name to the list."

"The pistol didn't match me."

"Didn't? You didn't get together with James until after we got the pistol."

"Is it true that you shot James?" Miss April said, as though she couldn't contain that question any longer.

Mabel bit her tongue, then she nodded. "Yes. That is true." She put up a finger. "But it was an accident. A true accident."

The ladies didn't look like they were sure whether or not they believed that. Thankfully James stepped in to her rescue.

"It was. She was taking the pistol out of the box and fumbled it a little bit. It went off and nipped me on my foot. Thankfully, Mabel used her doctoring skills to fix me up, and I'm good as new."

"Interesting story. Bet your children will love to hear that one."

"We haven't told it to them yet. We didn't want to scare them on their first day here," James said, winking.

The girls probably weren't the children that Miss April had meant, but Mabel appreciated the fact that James considered them their legitimate children.

"What are you going to add to the note?" Miss April asked, bringing the conversation back to the subject at hand.

"I haven't even seen the note. Once I handled the pistol and accidentally shot James, I didn't want to have anything to do with it. I put it back in the box, and I don't even know what Carol did with it."

"I put it in the kitchen on top of the shelf by the fridge. And I assumed we'd get back to it at some point." She smiled. "After all, that probably is something that we're going to want to pass along, isn't it?"

"I don't know. I... I guess it's true that right after the pistol came, I did get married, but it's also true that Billy was here in the yard, and Sweet Water often says that Billy is a matchmaking steer, so it could have been him."

"Maybe you are a tough nut to crack, and Billy and the pistol decided that it was going to take both of them." Miss April lifted her brows, as though that were a legitimate suggestion.

It made Mabel want to shake her head. A matchmaking pistol? A matchmaking steer? Both of them were preposterous.

Except, she couldn't deny the fact that she was now married, when she hadn't been a week ago.

The ladies were still there when Gladys, Mabel's sister, and her husband Silas and their children came to visit. Gladys laughed and said that she needed to get to know her nieces, because she wanted to have them stay at her house overnight.

The ladies left, and before Gladys and her husband left, they had played with the kids and arranged for the girls to go to their house and stay overnight the next weekend.

Mabel appreciated Gladys's offer. She had to admit that after all the events of the day, she was exhausted, and it wasn't even suppertime.

They'd fed the filly twice more, and Carol had gone in to start supper.

James moved from his perch where he had been leaning against the post most of the afternoon and came over and sat down on the porch swing as they watched Silas and Gladys's car fade out of sight.

"Busy day," he said casually as he sat down, putting his arm around her, and this time, he didn't let it lie on the back of the swing but set his hand casually on her shoulder, pulling her gently toward him.

"It sure was. My goodness, I don't know if it's the kids or the filly or the visitors, but I feel like it should be bedtime."

"I think we'll get our second wind. I hope so. I was kind of hoping we could talk to Aunt Carol. I don't want her cooking all the time for us if it's not something she wants to do."

"I don't want that either. Although, it's pretty obvious I'm going to have to take cooking lessons from someone if I'm going to take up cooking."

"I thought we talked about that. I'm going to take on the cooking. I wasn't talking about it as a hint for you, I was just wanting to make sure that you weren't going to be upset if Aunt Carol is in 'your' kitchen."

"Oh my goodness. I appreciate every single thing she has done, and I hope I thanked her profusely. Maybe I should thank her more."

"It's probably impossible to thank someone too much, but you really have been very appreciative and grateful. I hope I have too."

He tilted his head and ran his fingers down her arm and back up.

She contained her shiver as he said casually, "Are you sure you're okay with it?"

"I know. A woman's kitchen is her castle or whatever the saying is, but yes. I'm perfectly happy with another woman in the kitchen doing all the work." She laughed.

James laughed with her, and they swung together until Carol called them for supper.

When they went in, they set the table and sat down to some left-over chicken and some kind of noodle-based vegetable casserole that was delicious.

The girls looked windblown and happy, and they did not protest when James asked if everyone would stay at the table after they were done eating so they could talk a little bit about some of the arrangements they'd like to make.

In fact, the girls looked apprehensive and a little scared.

Mabel wanted to reassure them, but she didn't want to get the cart ahead of the horse, so instead, she said, "Maybe we can eat some cheesecake while we talk about it?"

The girls smiled at that, although Bernice still looked worried.

"We don't want to forget to feed Denise," Annabelle said as everyone sat down with dessert in front of them.

"Aunt Carol, maybe you can set your timer so that we don't go longer than forty-five minutes. That's how long we have until it's time for Denise to eat again," James said, smiling at Annabelle, who glowed under his approval.

Carol set her kitchen timer and came back to her seat.

"Now, I think this is mostly for the adults, but Mabel and I are hoping that the three of you will chime in with your opinions whenever you want to. We want to take them into consideration and make sure that everyone is happy with the way the house is being run. Now, of course, not everything we do is going to be exactly what you think we should do, and we can't do everything you want, but we totally want to take your opinions into consideration."

The girls looked unsure, as though they'd never been talked to by adults like that before.

"My first question is for Aunt Carol," James said after the girls didn't say anything.

"All right. I wondered where I was going to fit into this circus. Go ahead and tell me."

"Actually, I wanted you to tell me. I've already talked to Mabel, and she is perfectly fine if you take over any of the kitchen duties that you want. Mabel and I have decided that she will continue to work as a vet, and her family, that's me, Annabelle, Bernice, Caren, and Aunt Carol, will give her a hand when she needs it. That means we'll go on calls if she wants us to, and we'll also take care of most of the household chores. Of course, Mabel's going to pitch in when she can, but the cooking and the laundry and the cleaning will mostly be Aunt Carol, me, and the girls. Does that sound fair to you?"

"You mean we'll get to go with Miss Mabel when she goes to help people with their animals?" Bernice said, like she couldn't quite believe it.

"You sure will. That was the whole point. We want you to be able to help. You're part of this family, and while families are supposed to be fun, there's also a lot of work involved, and that includes the cooking and cleaning and also taking care of animals."

The girls looked like they weren't sure how to process that, and they also seemed like they were too apprehensive to be as happy as they wanted to be.

"So you're asking me if I want to do all the cooking?" Carol said.

"I'm asking you how much of the cooking you want to do. How much of the other work you want to do. We don't want to throw everything on you and have it be too much."

"I think I'd like to make all the meals, and someone else can do the laundry and cleaning. I'll be in charge of the dishes and the table, although you want the girls to have chores that they're in charge of, right?"

"I sure do. And if you'll be in charge of making sure they do any of the kitchen chores we assign them, including dishes and cooking, then that would be great."

"Cook? You want me to cook?" Annabelle said, like the idea was foreign to her.

"Would you be interested in learning to cook?" Carol asked.

"I can make spaghetti," Annabelle said, like that was something to be proud of. "Then I can put hot dogs in it, and if you have peas, put peas in it, too, because Mom said that makes it healthy."

Well, they were going to have their work cut out teaching the girls what actual healthy food was, but maybe having a garden would help with that. That was a project for next year though. It was a little late to try to get started this year. Although, they could probably prepare the ground.

"I think you can put gardening on the list of things we're going to do."

"You mean like grow plants? Because we grew bean plants in kindergarten. But when I took it home, it died," Caren said, like kindergarten was a long time ago or something. He was pretty sure that she had just completed it last year.

Of course, to a seven-year-old, two years was a long time ago.

They continued to discuss the jobs that they would be willing to do, the things that they felt they were good at, and the things that they were interested in. Mabel was happy that James did not insist that the girls only do what they wanted to do, but that he would slant the chores in the favor of the girls' interests and lighten their load in the areas where they weren't as eager to help.

Although, everyone had to learn to scrub the toilets and clean the bathrooms, and no one was going to only get to do exactly what they wanted to.

Mabel figured that was a pretty good example of what real life was, since even if a person loved their job, there were parts of their job they really didn't always enjoy. Or parts of their job that were sometimes hard.

All in all, it was a productive meeting, and as the kitchen timer went off, and they got up to go feed Denise, she felt that even if they didn't stick to everything that they decided, they accomplished their main goal, which was making the girls feel like they were part of the family.

Chapter 21

O n a Saturday evening several weeks later, they gathered around the table after the girls had been settled in for the night.

"It's high time we open this pistol case and see exactly what it says."

Carol had not taken no for an answer, and while Mabel didn't want to ever touch the pistol again, she agreed with James that it was better to educate herself and face her fears. She'd already signed up for shooting lessons from Ames Palmer, who offered them at the Olympic training center just outside of Sweet Water.

Still, her hands trembled as she clasped them on the table in front of her while Carol set the rich-looking case down in front of her. James sat beside her, his steady presence giving her strength and calm as she took a deep breath

"After you open it, I have a paper that the woman who told me about it gave me. She did some research on it."

"A paper?" Mabel asked, her hands stilling on the clasp.

"It has some information on it about the other owners of the gun."

"Oh." Mabel assumed they must have gotten married, too? She wasn't sure.

Her fingers trembled as she undid the clasp and carefully opened the case, showing the pink-handled pistol that lay nestled in the deep velvet lining. It was a bit worn, but nothing like she would have expected for a piece that was more than a hundred years old.

Without touching the pistol, she gently fingered the lining, feeling goose bumps rise up on her arms at the thought of touching something that belonged to Annie Oakley. Maybe it was the thought of all the women who came after. Strong women who found love, just like she had.

Only she hadn't told James she loved him.

He'd worked alongside her, as her assistant, with Denise, with the girls, and doing the household chores. He'd supported her in everything she did. Which, of course, made her try to do everything she could to support him. All he seemed to want was to spend time with her and the girls. It made her heart happy.

Feeling something crinkle under her fingers, she found a small pocket and pulled out two pieces of paper.

Carefully, she opened the first one and spread it out on the table, reading aloud.

She who possesses this pistol possesses an opportunity that must not be squandered. Cast in the tender dreams of maidens from ages past, the steel of this weapon is steadfast and true and will lead an unmarried woman to a man forged from the same virtuous elements. One need only fit her hand to the grip and open her heart to activate the promise for which this pistol was fashioned—the promise of true love. Patience and courage will illuminate her path. Hope and faith will guide her steps until her heart finds its home.

Once the promise is fulfilled, the bearer must release the pistol and pass it to another or risk losing what she has found.

Accept the gift...or not.

Believe its promise...or not.

But hoard the pistol for personal gain...and lose what you hold most dear.

Mabel tried to swallow, but her throat felt like sandpaper.

It very well could be a matchmaking pistol. She raised her eyes slowly and met James's gaze. There was so much in his eyes. So much tenderness and compassion, so much admiration and love.

She looked back down, touching her fingers to the handle of the pistol before she wrapped them around it, willing herself to not be afraid.

As she gripped the gun, careful to point it away from any bodies, it seemed to warm her hand and create a trail of warmth that went straight to her heart.

"I love you," she said suddenly, looking right at James. The words ripped out. She couldn't hold them in even if she wanted to, which she didn't.

He smiled, a full, happy smile, but one that held no surprise. "I love you. I have forever."

"I'm sorry I'm a slow learner."

"I don't think you're slow. Everything happened in the perfect time. In God's perfect time."

She nodded because he was totally and completely correct.

"Are we going to look at the other paper?" he asked, prompting her to remember that they were sitting at the kitchen table, the pistol case open and Carol patiently waiting.

"Uh, yes. Of course," she stuttered, carefully folding the first sheet of paper and putting it back in the case.

"I think the information I have goes with the other paper," Carol said, taking a long, white envelope out of her purse and carefully pulling several sheets of handwritten papers out, unfolding them and laying them on the table in front of her.

Mabel tucked the first paper back and gently lifted the second one out, flattening it on the table as well. It contained assorted styles of handwriting. Some bold and thick, others thin and classy.

It seemed she would be adding her own handwriting to the sheet.

The idea made nerves coil in her stomach. She ignored them and read the first line.

"A gift from the great Annie Oakley, this pistol carries a legacy of love. If you possess this pistol and find love, please record your name and a bit of your story to encourage those who follow."

"It did belong to Annie!" she couldn't help but exclaim. She hadn't been sure, even though it's what she'd been told. Everything took on a newer and more meaningful cadence.

She cleared her throat and read the first entry.

"Tessa James married Jackson Spivey on March 3, 1894, in Caldwell, Texas—I was aiming for his heart but accidentally winged him in the arm. Thankfully, forgiveness and love cover a multitude of mishaps."

"Sounds like someone needed a sense of humor," James interjected.

"Let me read to you what my friend found out about this couple." Carol ignored the smiles that James and Mabel shared as she began to read from her sheet.

"According to an article in the Caldwell *Register* from 1894, Tessa Spivey claimed to have received the pistol as a gift from Annie Oakley after taking lessons from the famous sharpshooter down in Austin. When asked why she'd wanted to learn to shoot, Mrs. Spivey admitted that it had been a ploy to gain the attention of her soon-to-be husband. Jackson Spivey had been living under the shadow of his disreputable father at the time and had demonstrated no interest in courtship. His father, Mr. Sam Spivey, was known to be a drunkard, gambler, and all-around wastrel and had been incarcerated at the state penitentiary in Huntsville. Left to make his own way in the world, Jackson put his skills with a rifle to good use, bringing in fresh game for the local hotel and working in Caldwell's lone gun shop. Miss James worked for a dressmaker of some renown, a Mrs. Elliott, and recalled Mr. Spivey's reticence toward her. 'I never thought to need an actual gun for husband hunting,' she said in the article, 'but Jackon left me little choice. I thought my taking up shooting would build common ground between us, but it nearly ended our relationship before it started.'"

Carol scanned her notes. "According the same article, Tessa later used the pistol to help foil a robbery."

"Oh! It sounds dangerous. Is that all there is?" Mabel asked, biting her lip.

"There's a mention of her giving the pistol to her friend Laura Marshall after she married Jackson. It seems that Laura didn't use the pistol herself but passed it along to her cousin, a Miss Rena Burke."

""Ooo, that's the second one!" Mabel said, wanting to skip ahead and find out about all the women at once. She felt a deep sense of sisterhood with Tessa, despite the fact that they were separated by more than a century of time. It was an odd feeling but one she loved.

"You read what you have," Carol instructed.

"Rena Burke wed Josh Gatlin on June 2, 1894, in Holiday, Oregon. When my trousers and target practice didn't send him running, I knew true love had hit the perfect target for me."

"Trousers?" James asked.

"That's what they called pants back then."

"I guess your trousers haven't sent me running, either."

"I haven't started my target practice yet."

He laughed.

Carol ignored them again and read from her paper. "Desperate for a fresh start, Rena Burke journeys from Texas to Oregon with only her father's pistol and a plodding old mule for company. She takes a job working with explosives at a mine, spends her free time emulating her hero Annie Oakley, and secretly longs to be loved.

"Saddlemaker Josh Gatlin has one purpose in life, and that is his daughter. Gabi is his joy and the sunshine in his days. Then he meets a trouser-wearing woman living life on her own terms.

Rena is nothing like his perception of what he wants in a wife and mother for his child, but she might just prove to be everything he needs."

"That's interesting. Now the pistol is in Oregon. Wasn't it in Texas to begin with?" James puckered his brows.

"I think that's part of the allure of the pistol. No one is quite sure how it turns up when it does." Carol didn't seem fazed by the large amount of traveling the pistol had done.

"It would be neat to see that on a map," Mabel mused.

"Let's read the rest of this, then maybe I can work on doing that," James offered. "If not tonight, then as I have time. I'd like to see it too."

"Okay." Mabel loved that idea.

"Next," Carol commanded.

"Kristalee Donovan wed Captain Johnny Houston on August 31, 1899, in Hugo, Indian Territory. With a little help from the pink pistol, both of us learned what love really is and will treasure that love forever. How new and bright life has suddenly become. Can there be any adventure more wonderful than this?" Mabel looked up. "How romantic! That describes the way I feel about my life—how new and bright it has suddenly become!" Her shining eyes met James's. The feeling of sisterhood strengthened in her soul. She could see why someone might be tempted to want to keep the pistol. It gave her the feeling of community.

"What do you have about this one?" James asked Carol. But she was already getting ready to read.

"Beautiful Krissy Donovan, a student of Annie Oakley, is asked to put on a sharpshooting benefit for an orphanage. The trouble is, it's half a continent away. Her father has promised her services, and she finds herself virtually alone in perilous Indian Territory. Krissy's father realizes he has made a terrible mistake, but a cavalry scout, familiar with the savage land, is the only one who can protect Krissy now.

"Rough-and-tumble cavalry captain Johnny Houston resents being asked to take on this last assignment of playing nursemaid to an eastern debutante before he musters out of the army. Johnny understands his duty as a soldier, so turning the order down is out of the question. With a killer stalking them, Johnny has to keep his mind on Krissy's safety, but an attraction to his stubborn charge could end up compromising his heart.

"Memories of his own harsh childhood at the same orphanage haunt him. He has no choice but to make a stand for the children, or some of them won't survive. Krissy dares to hope she can help in some way, even though it means giving up the lavish future that has been planned for her since birth."

"Wow. She was a student of Annie Oakley. Can you imagine?" Mabel said with reverence. How she wished she could meet the great sharpshooter as well.

"You'll be taking lessons from Ames Palmer. She has an Olympic gold medal in shooting, although I'm sure it's not the same." James grinned.

"I actually heard that she and Palmer got together because of their shooting competitions. Or maybe it was because of their broken legs. I can't really remember what exactly I heard." Carol scratched her head, then nodded at Mabel. "Give us the next one."

"Goldie Colson wed Rhys Miller on August 31, 1900. I thought the pink pistol I found would save my life. It saved my heart instead. Okay, it could have saved my life too, but only because I have good aim."

"Ha! Another one with a sense of humor." James grinned.

Mabel loved that he seemed to be enjoying this, because she was loving it, but she would have quit if he were bored.

"This one was right at the turn of the century. Wow," Mabel mused.

"Here's what I have," Carol began. "Goldie Colson has lost everything, including her parents, in a fire. So, she does what any other woman would do in her predicament. She becomes a mail-order bride. Unfortunately, before she can tie the knot, she loses her betrothed and his father to train robbers! Now she's stuck in Nowhere, Washington, with nothing but the two men's meager belongings, including a pistol her future father in-law found. Considering she shot one of the train robbers, it might come in handy if she ever ran into them again.

"Rhys Miller couldn't complain about his life. He was best friends with some of the Weavers of the famous Weaver Farm and enjoyed working at the town's only bank, even if it was a little dull. Then *she* came to town, and Rhys didn't know if he was coming or going. Goldie Colson was scared and rightly so. Strangers were asking after her at the Weaver Farm, and after hearing about what happened to her with a bunch of train robbers, a few of them might want her dead. But Rhys isn't sure which is worse, guarding Goldie from danger or guarding his heart from her."

"Train robbers? I thought those only appeared in westerns, not in real life." James studied the pistol. "It seems like this pistol has been through more than I thought."

"Me too. I can't believe the stories it could tell if it could talk." Mabel lifted her eyes to James. "It could tell one about us."

They smiled at each other.

"It sure could," he murmured.

"Let's read the rest of these. There might be even more excitement. We've only gone through four. There are ten owners before you." Carol had each one numbered on her paper.

"Okay. Here's my Pink Pistol Sister number five." Mabel smiled, loving the name she'd dubbed her fellow pistol owners. How sweet it would be to meet these interesting women of the past!

"Kitty Horwath married Thad Easton this 25th of December, the year of our Lord 1910. A competition in Deadwood pitted us against each other, but a last-minute challenge and a test of faith won my heart (and the prize)."

"Deadwood? That's in South Dakota!" James exclaimed.

"It took ten years for it to show up again," Mabel mused.

"When Kitty's father disappears, she and her family must find a way to pay for their house.

"Another payment missed and they lose everything. Kitty has one shot to save them, the winning prize would earn her freedom from a dastardly uncle, if only she had the chance to make it.

"Thad is setting up the Deadwood annual shooting tournament and thinks he's solved Kitty's problem by setting up a women's division. There's no prize, but she can compete. With her continued pressure, he realizes there's more to the story, but his hands are tied. If he allows a woman to compete against the men, all the donors could pull out and he would be a laughingstock."

"That's it?" James asked when Carol stopped.

"That's all she wrote." Carol lifted her hands.

"Even if she lost her house, they got married, so there was a happily ever after." Mabel personally would rather have her family than a house. It was just a building. Love was worth so much more.

"Interesting," Carol murmured.

James tapped the table thoughtfully. "I'd love to know more about their story. But also, where did the pistol go from there?"

Chapter 22

Mabel looked at her paper.

"Mine doesn't say where it went. I have Sharpshooter Violet Taylor married Pastor Carson Davis on July 1, 1911. Keeping secrets threatened to ruin our shot at love. But when we found the courage to come clean to each other, the smoke cleared, and we were able to joyfully embrace what promises to be a bright future together."

"It's no good when couples keep secrets from each other." Mabel was firm in this. Sometimes things were hard to talk about, but a relationship needed trust and openness in order to survive.

"I'm not sure mine says where they were, either. It says, Violet Taylor leads a double life. She performs in a traveling show as the mysterious Masked Marvel, a daring and commanding sharpshooter. But in real life, she holds back and allows others to lead the way. When an accident puts her arm in a sling, she has to scramble to protect the secret of her identity as the Masked Marvel. So she enlists the help of her identical twin sister, a 'townie' dressmaker, to secretly swap places until her arm heals. But that means she must also take on her sister's role as director of a children's church program. There's just one hitch. Her sister's sweet on Pastor Carson, the program's codirector, so Violet has to make sure not to mess anything up with him.

"Pastor Carson Davis became guardian to an orphaned nine-year-old six months ago and has been struggling to build a relationship with the boy ever since. It's to the point where he's begun to wonder if he's even fit to be a pastor. Could finding himself a wife who'd be a proper mother figure for his foster son be the solution?

"As Violet and Carson work together on the children's program, the attraction between them grows. But awareness of her sister's feelings and guilt over her deception hold Violet back.

"Little does she know that Carson is harboring secrets of his own..."

Carol looked over the paper. "Oh, here it says the pistol was in Larkin, Missouri."

"Missouri?" James exclaimed. "It's traveling south. There doesn't seem to be any rhyme or reason about how it gets to where it goes."

"That does seem to be a mystery. Although it might have happened like it did for us—Carol brought it when she moved from Oklahoma. Maybe it was sent with an aunt or other relative who wanted to see their charges married."

"Or their nephews." Carol smiled.

"Okay, here is Pink Pistol Sister number seven," Mabel intoned. "Mariah Bartee finally succumbed to Dax Talon's charms and married him on the first day of spring, March 20, 1940. She traded danger and secrets she'd known for much of her life for security and love. It was a peaceful new beginning for both."

"Sounds like she had a hard life," Carol mused.

"It was 1940. Not an easy time for anyone. Wasn't that coming out of the Great Depression?" James asked.

"Yes. The stock market crashed in 1929, so that was just eleven years later." She took a breath. "Here is what she found for them. The challenge of raising her siblings is one Mariah Bartee willingly bears. She'll keep them together at all costs—and safe from the danger lurking on the mountain. A handsome stranger's arrival raises the stakes when he asks for her help. She doesn't trust easily.

"Dax Nolan, a cowboy from the lowlands, hesitates to involve Mariah, but no one knows the mountains like her. Desperation drives him. Can the bones recently uncovered be his missing sister?

"Mariah reluctantly agrees to guide Dax, and they encounter danger and secrets. As they search for truth, she finds herself falling for him. He can offer security—and love. And," Carol added, "before you can ask, the note says the pistol was in Boulder, Colorado. A long way from Missouri!"

"I can't wait to make a map for it, even though it's obvious there is no set guidelines for how long the pistol goes between owners and where it might show up next."

"Speaking of showing up next, here is the next one. Rexanna Brennan married Roan Bertoletti on September 29, 1955. I've shot exotic game worthy of the finest of trophies, but my cowboy's love has been my biggest prize of all."

"She was a big game hunter? The pistol doesn't seem to care whether the woman knows how to shoot or not, since this woman was a hunter and I've never shot a gun before." Mabel was trying to find a link between them, if not time or location, then personality, but that didn't seem to matter, either.

"Mine says, After a devastating loss, wild game hunter Rexanna Brennan returns home to her family's ranch to heal. She never expects to learn her crazy aunt has left her a pink pistol with an even crazier legend. But more unsettling, a Hollywood cowboy has moved onto the ranch, stealing her family's hearts and maybe her legacy, too.

"False accusations throw Roan Bertoletti into scandal and yank him out of his movie star life. His reputation shredded, he grasps at the second chance the Brennan family gives him. With his roots firmly planted, he's living his dream to be a cowboy again, and he has no plans to leave the ranch anytime soon.

"But Rexanna's grief pulls at him. So does her insistence she can't stay. Can he convince the beautiful heiress to claim what has always been hers?"

"He must have been able to persuade her," James said with a grin. "I can feel a kinship with this dude—wanting to be a cowboy and talking the girl into falling for him."

"You didn't have to talk me into anything," Mabel chided, but mostly because she felt bad that it had taken her so long to notice him. Still, the fact that she noticed him in God's perfect timing couldn't be disputed. Everything had come together so perfectly. Maybe that's what they all had in common. The pistol had shown up at the perfect time in their life.

"Is there another?" James asked.

"There are two more," Carol said. "Mabel?"

"Grace Marshall wed Levi Gibson amid autumn's splendor on October 15, 1972. He called me a lucky shot, but what I really am is lucky in love to marry the man I love with all my heart and soul."

"That's romantic," Carol said with her hand over her heart. Then she looked down at her own paper. "As a registered nurse at the Boise VA Hospital, Grace Marshall is devoted to her patients, but some wounds require more than medical care. A patient too stubborn and angry to accept the help he needs storms out of her exam room, ruffling her feathers. Yet, when the man returns to apologize, something about him tugs at her heart.

"Levi Gibson left for war young and idealistic but returned from Vietnam with physical scars and a haunted soul. He tries to banish the darkness brewing inside him with hard work on his family's potato farm, but it's a young nurse's kindness that brings unexpected light and joy into his life. If Levi can open up to Grace and let her see his pain, could she be the key that unlocks a future full of hope instead of mere survival?

"After her father sends Grace a legendary pistol, target practice provides an excuse to spend time with Levi during the summer of

1972. As his shadows overwhelm him, it will take far more than a lucky shot for Grace to hit love's mark."

"A nurse and a soldier."

"The year was 1972. Then the pistol disappears for more than fifty years." Carol tapped her paper. "The next time it surfaces, it's with this woman's niece." She glanced at Mabel. "Did she write something on the paper?"

"Yes. Josephine Jade Buchanan married Dalton Matthew Kelley on April 29, 2023, in Loksi, Oklahoma. The inheritance from my beloved aunt enriched my life in unimaginable ways by giving me a second shot at love and a home. This time, I'm holding onto my Oklahoma cowboy and the priceless gift of a future with him."

"We all know how the pistol made it from Oklahoma to North Dakota."

"They weren't even married when she sent the pistol to us."

"I don't think they need to keep it until they're married. Just until they find love. They probably wrote the wedding date down when they knew it."

"Oh, that makes sense."

"I want to hear about the woman who just had it." James motioned to the paper in front of Carol, indicating she needed to read.

She didn't need a second push. "Childhood disappointments and a bitter divorce taught Jade Buchanan that trusting her heart to a man leads to disaster. When she returns to Oklahoma to settle her aunt's estate, Jade discovers the cowboy hired to renovate the house is none other than Dalton Kelley, her first love. She's not worried, though. She has a solid plan—supervise the renovation like the adult she is, sell the property, and return to New York City with money to start a design company with her best friend. Simple. Until she starts working with Dalton and feelings she thought long dead bubble to the surface, raising havoc with her carefully laid plans.

"Needing money thanks to cattle rustlers, Dalton hires on to renovate Jade's recently inherited house. Working for his teenage sweetheart will be awkward, but he can handle it in the short term. He'll collect his money, say goodbye to Jade, and find a woman without big-city dreams to settle down with on his Done Roamin' Ranch. But the job brings trouble he hadn't counted on, and the more time he and Jade spend together, the less he can picture any other woman by his side."

"I'd love to get in touch with them—a real Pink Pistol Sister who is still alive. Wouldn't that be neat?" Mabel grinned at James.

"And we could talk to her aunt. The one who put all of this together. Maybe she's uncovered more details. Or at least she might have ideas of what direction we could go to start digging." Mabel ran a finger over the pink pistol. It had brought eleven couples together and changed those lives completely.

"What are you going to write about you and James?" Carol asked.

"Oh, goodness. I hadn't even thought of that."

"You should. Then you ought to figure out how to pass it on. I don't want to take any chances on losing what we have." James grinned at her, and she had no choice but to return his smile.

"Oh, look at the time!" Carol exclaimed. "I'd better get to bed if I'm going to get up and get breakfast going at a decent hour in the morning."

She folded her paper, handing it to Mabel to tuck into the gun case, and excused herself for the night.

"I still need to feed Denise." Mabel snapped the case closed and pushed back away from the table. James stood with her and carefully set the gun case on the high shelf beside the refrigerator.

He turned back slowly to face her, still not saying anything.

"James?"

"Hmm?"

"Are you okay?" She hoped all the information about the gun hadn't scared him or anything. Although she couldn't imagine why it would have.

"I'm fine." He stepped closer. "But I did want to ask you something."

"Okay?" she breathed, her lungs freezing up as he didn't stop until he was directly in front of her, his arms sliding around her back and his head lowering until his lips were beside her ear.

"You said you loved me."

"And you said you loved me," she returned, sliding her arms around his waist and smiling. She loved it when he held her and spoke in her ear, sending shivers all the way from her head to her toes.

"You meant it?" he asked, like he truly didn't know.

"I did." She took a breath, her lungs still not wanting to work properly. "I... I was hoping...hoping maybe you might be interested in getting a roommate?"

His lips had been trailing down her temple, but they froze and his whole body went still. "I hope you're not thinking of moving Denise into my room to make it easier to feed her at night."

"No. I wasn't thinking about Denise at all."

"Hmm. Then, yeah, I might be interested. Who would my roommate be?"

Like he didn't know.

"Me?"

"Ah, Mabel. You don't know how long I've waited to hear you say that. Are you sure? Because I can't be noble about it."

"I'm sure. I've been sure for a while, I just didn't know how to say it to you."

"Say, James, you can finally have what you've wanted for years."

"Really?"

"To kiss you like I want to? To hold you all night long? To have you want me? Yeah. Really." His lips trailed across her jaw and up to the corner of her mouth. "If we go out and take care of Denise, you're not going to change your mind, are you?" he breathed.

"No. I told you, I've wanted this for a while but just didn't...realize how much you wanted it too. We were both suffering, I guess."

"Suffering. Now there's a word that does not describe me—a man who has every single thing he's ever wanted in life."

"After tonight, that will be me, too."

"After tonight?"

"Of course. Being with you is the only thing I need after the girls and the family we've made."

"Even being a vet?"

"I don't want to give that up, but if I had to, it would be easy."

"I love you."

"I love you, too. Now, how fast do you think we can feed Denise?"

"I think I want to kiss you first."

"You have the best ideas."

His head lowered, their lips touched, and Denise had to wait a rather long time for her next meal.

End note: *Mabel Lefrak married James Mannon on Tuesday, June 13, 2023. Before the pistol came into my possession, I was alone, but because of God's grace and goodness, and a small accident, I gained a man I love more than life, and three girls—a ready-made family that is Pistol Perfect.*

If you love the town of Sweet Water, North Dakota and would like to read more about it, Jessie has three whole series set there. The book that started it all, *The Cowboy's Best Friend*, Book 1 in the Sweet Water Ranch Western Cowboy Romance series is . If you'd like to learn more about Jessie, get a free book and find out about sales and specials and new releases, sign up for her newsletter .

Enjoy this preview of *The Cowboy's Best Friend,* just for you!

The Cowboy's Best Friend

Chapter 1

"So, Ames, you gonna go shooting with me?" Palmer Olson asked, hooking a thumb in the front pocket of his jeans, his eyes shielded from the North Dakota sun by his cowboy hat.

Ames Hanson flashed a quick grin, her mind whirling, already thinking of the race-and-shoot-targets course they'd always used. "We racing?" she asked.

"Of course," he replied with the corners of his mouth tilted up and a glance at the two four-wheelers he had out and ready.

She needed a head start if she had any hope of beating him. His machine was bigger than hers, although her aim was better. It had been eighteen months since she'd seen her best friend. He might fall for the oldest trick in the book.

She gasped. "Holy smokes! Look at that!" She pointed at the sky behind him. "Is that a bald eagle?"

She chuckled as he turned, falling for her ruse. There wasn't a cloud in the sky. Not a bird, either.

As soon as he turned, she spun and raced to the four-wheelers. He already had their rifles on the racks, the ammo strapped down beside them. She jumped on hers, started it, and gunned the motor.

Behind her, she could hear him shouting. Something about not being fair or some such nonsense.

What wasn't fair was that he had more power under his seat than she did. That's what wasn't fair. But it was his ranch, his machines. He'd had the same one since before they graduated from high school eleven years ago. She'd actually had the same one as well. His old machine.

She couldn't complain. Not every girl was blessed with a best friend whose family owned a thousand-acre ranch in North Dakota. Actually, in all her world travels, she'd never met anyone else with that benefit. Palmer was a one-of-a-kind guy, and she regretted all the time she'd taken their friendship for granted.

He hadn't caught up to her by the time she hit the bend in the road where it cut behind the corral and angled up between two hundred-acre fields.

The four-wheeler cornered the turn on two wheels. Ames hunkered down, lowering the center of gravity and leaning her body into the turn. The wide blue North Dakota sky soared above her as she came out of the curve, the road straightening and arrowing off into the flat distance. The ATV bounced back down. She pressed the throttle wide open. After a one-second lag time, the motor screamed, and the four-wheeler jumped ahead. Flat rows of flax and a deep green carpet of wheat flew by as she raced up the middle.

Tempted to turn and look to see if Palmer was catching her, she kept her gaze straight ahead. As fast as she was going, a little tilt of the wheel could make her spin out of control. Part of going this fast was knowing what boundaries she could push.

The wind whipped through her hair, and she couldn't keep the happy smile off her face. LA was great. Hiking in the Himalayas was fabulous, and winning two Olympic gold medals was awesome, but nothing compared to being home.

She heard Palmer before she saw him. He might have a bigger machine, but he was heavier. Actually, now that she thought about it, it looked like he'd gained weight. Not around the middle, but his shoulders were much broader than she remembered. His biceps bigger. She always thought of him as this skinny guy from high school, but as she'd been living her dreams out in the world, he'd been here on the ranch, running it with his brother and sister and obviously doing enough physical labor in the process to add a pile of muscle to his lanky frame.

The screaming of his machine grew louder, and he crept into her peripheral vision. The road was straight, the ground flat, but at the speeds they were going now, it would be foolish for her to turn her head to see how close he was. Focusing on keeping the handlebars steady, she pressed the accelerator with her thumb, ignoring the burning in the side of her hand. The competitor in her couldn't give up.

He was beside her now on the dirt road. She didn't have to turn her head to know what his face looked like. He'd be smiling, of course. But there would also be that little furrow between his brows. The one that he always had when they competed. She'd practiced for hundreds of hours to win gold in the biathlon at the Olympics, but there was absolutely no question that Palmer was the main reason she stood on the top podium. His face was the one she saw as the flag was raised and she had her hand over heart as the anthem of her country played. He never gave quarter.

Always having the smaller ATV had caused her to become a better shooter. Flat-out racing had improved her concentration and ability to handle her rifle despite the adrenaline coursing through her body.

What Palmer and she did here on the ranch in the summer wasn't close to an actual winter Olympic biathlon race where racers skied to each target that they had to aim at and shoot, although she and Palmer did race on skis when she was home in the winter. They didn't do the shooting the same either. But it didn't matter. Her competitions with Palmer had given her the grit she needed to win.

Their makeshift shooting range was just ahead. She crouched behind the handlebars, trying to wring out every ounce of aerodynamics she could.

She didn't give an inch when he locked the tires and fishtailed the rear end, stopping right in front of the range. She slid around to a stop right beside him and was only a second behind him grabbing her rifle and ammo off the rack.

They always shot this one in the prone position, wrists not touching the ground. On a good day, she could load her single-shot, lever-action .22 in 4.3 seconds. Palmer was about two seconds slower.

Drawing herself in, calming her muscles and heart, she steadied her breath. At the Olympics, she was never the fastest skier on the course. This is where she made up her time. She could calm her body, and she never missed a shot, loading her rifle faster and shooting more accurately than anyone else.

She gently squeezed the trigger on the first shot. Fifty meters downrange, in the middle of the green wheat field, her first 4.5 cm target disappeared.

Four more shots downed the other four targets. This wasn't an Olympic race, and as she rose to her feet and raced to her four-wheeler, she gloated at Palmer, "Ha! Eat dust, *Cowboy.*"

Hooking her rifle on, she started her four-wheeler and gunned it toward the next makeshift shooting range.

Again, Palmer caught her just before the range, and again, she outshot him, this time from a standing position. The targets were slightly bigger, but it never mattered to her. She could hit anything she could see. The first time.

The road followed the rectangular field, and she took the last corner on two wheels, heading back toward the barn. Halfway between the corner and the barn, she skidded to a stop at the last homemade shooting range. This time, she'd beaten Palmer there, and that almost guaranteed her win.

She kept her concentration, though, as she yanked her rifle out and jumped off the four-wheeler. Palmer skidded to a stop beside her. Close. So close, she thought he was going to hit her, and she committed the cardinal sin: she looked at him.

Normally, in any professional race, she wouldn't even acknowledge that she had competitors. She raced like she had blinders on.

However, the competitors skied, or a few times, she'd competed in the summer equivalent of a biathlon where the competitors jogged. She'd never had to worry about an overeager competitor hitting her with his ATV.

Palmer didn't hit her, but the damage was done. It wasn't that she looked at him, per se. It was more about *what* he looked like. His plain white t-shirt clung lovingly to shoulders as wide as cross members on electric wires. His biceps bulged as he grabbed his rifle. His long, jean-clad legs flexed with power and strength as he leapt off the four-wheeler and raced to get in position.

He threw himself on the ground, stretched out, rifle ready. Broad shoulders tapered to a narrow waist, and his boots, worn and scuffed, pointed back toward her. He'd long since lost his cowboy hat, and his hair was only slightly longer than the stubble on his face.

In those two seconds she looked at him, it hit her for the first time in her life. Palmer was rugged. Tough. Handsome.

Attractive.

That thought was what made her stumble.

It was a rogue. There was no way she could think like that. Palmer was her best friend.

She flung herself down on the ground beside him, lifting her rifle. It would take him seven shots to hit the five targets. That meant she had nine seconds on him, since she would hit all of hers, and he'd waste those nine seconds reloading twice more than she would have to.

Except...she missed.

Frustration rocked through her. She missed maybe five percent of her shots. Maybe. On a day she had the flu. Today, with the sun shining down and her in perfect health, she couldn't believe it.

It only took her a second to set her jaw and adjust her grip on the rifle. She didn't miss again, but Palmer must not have either, because he rose when she did, his targets all shot down, and raced to his machine.

They took off together, side by side, and flew wide open the last short distance to the far corral gate, which was always their unofficial finish line.

It wasn't enough for him to pull completely ahead of her. His body was even with her front tire. So, still holding the throttle wide open, she took her other hand off the handlebars and stretched out over her rifle, leaning forward as far as she could. Her fingertips just passed his handlebars as the gate flew closer.

She yelled, "I'm first, Cowboy!" as they flew by it, her fingertips just inching past him.

He turned at the sound of her voice. His eyes widened at her position. She probably looked like a bird on a death dive, but it didn't matter, because her fingers had crossed the line before any of his body parts.

She straightened on her ATV and punched her fist in the air. "Yahoo!" she cried.

Whatever little glitch she'd had at the last range was gone, and she turned brilliant eyes to Palmer. His shining blue eyes smiled back at her, even as he shook his head.

They hit the brakes, and their machines fishtailed in different directions, coming to a stop facing each other. How many hundreds of times over the years had they done this together? Maybe thousands since she'd decided in high school she wanted to compete in an Olympic biathlon.

Palmer had never wanted to be anything but a rancher on his grandparents' spread, but he'd been more than happy to help her get better.

"I won!" she said triumphantly, just in case he'd missed it.

"You did not. I was across the line well before you."

"Maybe. But my fingers broke the plane first, so that makes me the winner."

"All I had to do was scratch my nose, and my elbow would have been ahead of your fingers."

She tossed her hair. "Maybe you should have had an itchy nose, then."

"Fine. I'll let you say you won. This time."

"I win every time."

"No, you don't. I beat you once ten years ago, Squeegee."

Oh, he had to break the nickname out. She slapped her handlebars and crossed her arms over her chest. "That was the summer I had a broken leg and I let you talk me into racing anyway."

"I talked you into it, because I had a broken leg too." He lowered his head. "My broken leg was your fault, Squeegee."

Okay, so that was true. She'd thought bungee jumping from the top barn beam was a good idea, and she'd talked him into doing it with her, doubles. "How was I supposed to know the bungee cords would stretch like that?" After they'd been carted off to the hospital, both of them unable to walk, and after the pain meds had kicked in, he'd dubbed her Squeegee. She thought it was his way of combining Squashed and Bungee, but she wasn't sure. Sometimes with Palmer, she was better off not knowing.

Anyway, he didn't use it all the time but usually brought it out sometimes to remind her of her own stupidity. She wasn't falling for his mind games. "Why did you go along with it? No one made you jump off the top of the roof."

"Seriously? I was a loyal friend, and now, somehow everything is my fault?"

She tried not to react to the way he said "friend." She'd almost lost this race because of the inappropriate thoughts she'd been having about her "friend."

As though he knew she needed a subject change—Palmer could always read her mind—he said, "So, you're really back for the whole summer?"

"Yep." She kicked her legs up and propped her cowgirl boots on the handlebars, leaning back on her elbows and lifting her face to the big North Dakota sky. "There's not a sky in the world that compares to ours."

She heard him shift, but he didn't answer. He never seemed to care that she left for long periods of time since they'd graduated from high school. They texted all the time and facetimed week-ly—they joked about their Saturday night "facetime date."

She'd been to the Olympics, to the Himalayas, to all fifty states, and to seventeen different countries. She'd studied abroad, been runner-up in the Miss North Dakota contest, and worked in the corporate world as a marketing exec. All that time, Palmer had been a rock. Stuck on the farm. Content, apparently, with the short North Dakota summers and long, dark, frigid North Dakota winters.

"Working at the C Store?" he asked after a few minutes of them lying with their faces to the sky. That was the nice thing about Palmer. They didn't need to talk. And it didn't matter how long she'd been gone; they always picked right back up as best friends and buddies. It was never awkward. She wasn't even as close to any of her girlfriends as she was to him.

"Yeah." Her parents owned the only convenience store in Sweet Water. After coaching the junior world biathlon team all winter, she'd applied for and was now on the short list for a plum broad-casting job at a sports channel located in LA. She'd never lived very long anywhere since she'd left Sweet Water, and she was hoping to get that job and put down roots in the city.

"Staying this time?" he asked casually.

She didn't open her eyes or sit up. They'd talked about it when they were younger but hadn't had the conversation in a while. The one where he believed she would eventually come back and settle down, and she denied even liking North Dakota, let alone wanting to live here.

"No way." Her lips turned up in a grin, and she didn't even open her eyes. She knew what it took to set him off.

Only he didn't take the bait this time.

The silence between them stretched.

For the first time ever, she was uncomfortable with nothing between them, like if she didn't have words to anchor him to her, he'd drift off and she'd lose him. So she opened her mouth. "I told you about that job I applied for in LA. You ready to travel to California?"

The sun warmed her face and neck. She felt the heat through her jeans. But she felt the silence of her friend even more.

"Nah," he finally said. "Thinking I'm gonna get married."

Her eyes popped open. Her heart thudded to a stop, and her lungs froze.

She called on her Olympic training to keep from jerking up. Instead, she moved slowly, leveling her gaze at him before dropping her boots to the footrests and sitting up. "We text every day, and you didn't mention you had a girlfriend?"

Why wasn't she happy for him? Her brain felt scrambled, and she couldn't dredge up any good feelings at all. Which was weird, because she'd had two girlfriends in the past ten months announce their engagements, and Ames had been over the moon for them. Why wasn't she happier for Palmer?

He hadn't propped his feet up, but he was leaning back on his elbows. His thin white t-shirt allowed her to see, quite plainly, that his abs were well-defined. Her heart did that abnormal flip, and a thread of attraction wrapped around it. He lowered his eyes from the sky and looked at her under hooded lashes. "I don't."

Her stomach whipped back like she'd been hit in the midsection with a bowling ball. "Oh, my gosh. You're gay."

He grinned. Slow and easy, the grin she loved. The one he didn't use on anyone but her. "You think?"

She ran her eyes over his face, down his broad shoulders and deep chest, down to his waist where his jeans sat low on his hips. Her eyes flew back to his.

Why was she suddenly breathless?

"No, I don't. I guess we've never talked about that, though." They never talked about relationships. She'd not really had any. One didn't become an Olympic-caliber athlete by hanging out at bars, trying to pick up a date. Not that she'd even want to date a guy who didn't have anything else better to do with his time.

She decided to call his bluff. "So you have a boyfriend?" Her words didn't come out quite as confident and flippant as she wanted them to.

He did the slow grin on her again, and her heart flipped twice. When had Palmer gotten so handsome? And muscular?

"Nope."

"How long's it been since I've been home? Have we started a new tradition in Sweet Water where people just up and get married?"

"It's been eighteen months since you were here," he said. Answering her first question, but leaving her second one unanswered.

It had been winter. Palmer would have had a beard, and she probably wouldn't have seen him in anything less than a flannel shirt and lined vest. Insulated jeans and boots.

And before that, she'd come back for a few quick visits, so it had been years since they'd spent any large amounts of time together. At least five years or more since they'd spent the summer together. And now he goes and ruins it by announcing he was going to get married.

"You're only twenty-eight."

He shrugged.

"How are you getting married when you don't have a girlfriend?"

He shrugged again, the movements of his muscles under his t-shirt so fascinating she almost missed his answer.

"Figured you'd help me, Squeegee."

Pick up your copy of *The Cowboy's Best Friend* by Jessie Gussman today!

Manufactured by Amazon.ca
Acheson, AB